Welcome to Montana—the home of bold men
and daring women, where more than fifty tales
of passion, adventure and intrigue unfold
beneath the Big Sky. Don't miss a single one!

Montana ★MAVERICKS

DIANA PALMER
Rogue Stallion

Published by Silhouette Books
America's Publisher of Contemporary Romance

Special thanks and acknowledgment to Diana Palmer for her contribution to the Montana Mavericks series.

With appreciation and thanks to Marnie H. Pavelich for her contribution to the Montana Mavericks series.

 SILHOUETTE BOOKS
®

Recycling programs for this product may not exist in your area.

ISBN-13: 978-0-373-31023-4
ISBN-10: 0-373-31023-4

ROGUE STALLION

Visit Silhouette Books at www.eHarlequin.com

Printed in U.S.A.

DIANA PALMER

has a gift for telling the most sensual tales with charm and humor. With over forty million copies of her books in print, Diana Palmer is one of North America's most beloved authors and is considered one of the top ten romance authors in America.

One

There was a lull in Sheriff Judd Hensley's office, broken only by the soft whir of the fan. It sometimes amused visitors from back East that springtime in Whitehorn, Montana, was every bit as unpredictable as spring in the southeastern part of America, and that the weather could be quite warm. But the man sitting across the desk from Hensley was neither visitor nor was he amused. His dark, handsome face was wearing a brooding scowl, and he was glaring at his superior.

"Why can't the city police investigate? They have two detectives. I'm the only special investigator in the sheriff's department, and I'm overworked as it is," Sterling McCallum said, trying once more.

Hensley toyed with a pen, twirling it on the desk

absently while he thought. He was about the same build as McCallum, rugged and quiet. He didn't say much. When he did, the words meant something.

He looked up from the desk. "I know that," he said. "But right now, you're the one who deserves a little aggravation."

McCallum crossed his long legs and leaned back with a rough sigh. His black boots had a flawless shine, a legacy from his years in the U.S. Navy as a career officer. He had an ex-military mind-set that often put him at odds with his boss, especially since he'd mustered out with the rank of captain. He was much more used to giving orders than to taking them.

In the navy, the expected answer to any charge of dereliction of duty, regardless of innocence or guilt, was, "No excuse, sir." It was still hard for McCallum to get used to defending his actions. "I did what the situation called for," he said tersely. "When someone tries to pull a gun on me, I get twitchy."

"That was only bravado," Hensley pointed out, "and you knocked out one of his teeth. The department has to pay for it. The county commission climbed all over me and I didn't like it." He leaned forward with his hands clasped and gave the younger man a steady look. "Now you're the one with the problems. Dugin Kincaid found an abandoned baby on his doorstep."

"Maybe it's his," McCallum said with smiling sarcasm. Dugin was a pale imitation of his rancher father, Jeremiah. The thought of him with a woman amused McCallum.

"As I was saying," the sheriff continued without reacting to the comment, "the baby was found outside the city limits—hence our involvement—and its parents have to be found. You're not working on anything that pressing. You can take this case. I want you to talk with Jessica Larson at the social-welfare office."

McCallum groaned. "Why don't you just shoot me?"

"Now, there's no need to be like that," Hensley said, surprised. "She's a nice woman," he said. "Why, her dad was a fine doctor...."

His voice trailed off abruptly. McCallum remembered that Hensley's son had died in a hunting accident. Jessica's father had tried everything to save the boy, but it had been impossible. Hensley's wife, Tracy, divorced him a year after the funeral. That had happened years ago, long before McCallum left the service.

"Anyway, Jessica is one of the best social workers in the department," Hensley continued.

"She's the head of the department now, and a royal pain in the neck since her promotion," McCallum shot right back. "She's Little Miss Sunshine, spreading smiles of joy wherever she goes." His black eyes, a legacy from a Crow ancestor, glittered angrily. "She can't separate governmental responsibility from bleeding-heart activism."

"I wonder if it's fair to punish her by sticking her with

you?" Hensley asked himself aloud. He threw up his hands. "Well, you'll just have to grin and bear it. I can't sit here arguing with you all day. This is my department. I'm the sheriff. See this?" He pointed at the badge on his uniform.

"Needs polishing," McCallum noted.

Hensley's eyes narrowed. He stood up. "Get out of here before I forget you work for me."

McCallum unfolded his six-foot-plus length from the chair and stood up. He was just a hair taller than the sheriff, and he looked casual in his jeans and knit shirt and denim jacket. But when the jacket fell open, the butt of his .45 automatic was revealed, giving bystanders a hint of the sort of work he did. He was a plainclothes detective, although only outsiders were fooled by his casual attire. Most everyone in Whitehorn knew that McCallum was as conservative and military as the shine on his black boots indicated.

"Don't shoot anybody," Hensley told him. "And next time a man threatens to shoot you, check for a gun and disarm him before you hit him, please?" Hensley's eyes went to the huge silver-and-turquoise ring that McCallum wore on the middle finger of his right hand. "That ring is so heavy it's a miracle you didn't break his jaw."

McCallum held up his left hand, which was ringless. "This is the hand I hit him with."

"He said it felt like a baseball bat."

"I won't tell you where he hit *me* before he started

ranting about shooting," the detective replied, turning to the door. "And if I didn't work for you, a loose tooth would have been the least of his complaints."

"Jessica Larson is expecting you over at the social-services office," Hensley called.

McCallum, to his credit, didn't slam the door.

Jessica Larson was fielding paperwork and phone calls with a calmness that she didn't feel at all. She'd become adept at presenting an unflappable appearance while having hysterics. Since her promotion to social-services director, she'd learned that she could eat at her desk during the day and forgo any private life after work at night. She also realized why her predecessor had taken an early retirement. A lot of people came into this office to get help.

Like most of the rest of the country, Montana was having a hard time with the economy. Even though gambling had been legalized, adding a little more money to the state's strained coffers, it was harder and harder for many local citizens to make ends meet. Ranches went under all the time these days, forced into receivership or eaten up by big corporations. Manual labor, once a valuable commodity in the agricultural sector, was now a burden on the system when those workers lost jobs. They were unskilled and unemployable in any of the new, high-tech markets. Even secretaries had to use computers these days. So did policemen.

The perfunctory knock on her office door was emphasized by her secretary's high-pitched, "But she's busy…!"

"It's all right, Candy," Jessica called to the harassed young blonde. "I'm expecting McCallum." She didn't add that she hadn't expected him a half hour early. She tried to think of Sterling McCallum as a force of nature. He was like a wild stallion, a rogue stallion who traveled alone and made his own rules. Secretly, she was awed by him. He made her wish that she was a gorgeous model with curves in all the right places and a beautiful face—maybe with blond hair instead of brown. At least she was able to replace her big-rimmed glasses with contacts, which helped her appearance. But when she had allergies, she had to wear the glasses…like right now.

McCallum didn't wait for her to ask him to sit down. He took the chair beside her desk and crossed one long leg over the other.

"Let's have it," he said without preamble, looking unutterably bored.

Her eyes slid over his thick dark hair, so conventionally cut, down to his equally dark eyebrows and eyes in an olive-tan face. He had big ears and big hands and big feet, although there was nothing remotely clumsy about him. He had a nose with a crook in it, probably from being broken, and a mouth that she dreamed about: very wide and sexy and definite. Broad shoulders tapered to a broad chest and narrow hips like a rodeo rider's. His stomach was flat and he had long, muscular legs. He was so masculine that he made her ache. She was twenty-five, a mature woman and only about ten years younger than he was, but he made her feel childish sometimes, and inadequate—as a professional and as a woman.

"Hero worship again, Jessica?" he chided, amused by her soft blush.

"Don't tease. This is serious," she chided gently in turn.

He shrugged and sighed. "Okay. What have you done with the child?"

"Jennifer," she told him.

He glowered. "The abandoned baby."

She gave up. He wouldn't allow anyone to become personalized in his company. Boys he had to pick up were juvenile delinquents. Abandoned babies were exactly that. No names. No identity. No complications in his ordered, uncluttered life. He let no one close to him. He had no friends, no family, no connections. Jessica felt painfully sorry for him, although she tried not to let it show. He was so alone and so vulnerable under that tough exterior that he must imagine was his best protection from being wounded. His childhood was no secret to anyone in Whitehorn. Everyone knew that his mother had been an alcoholic and that, after her arrest and subsequent death, he had been shunted from foster home to foster home. His only real value had been as an extra hand on one ranch or another, an outsider always looking in through a cloudy window at what home life might have been under other circumstances.

"You're doing it again," he muttered irritably.

Her slender eyebrows lifted over soft brown eyes. "What?" she asked.

"Pigeonholing me," he said. "Poor orphan, tossed from pillar to post…"

"I wish you'd stop reading my mind," she told him. "It's very disconcerting."

"I wish you'd stop bleeding all over me," he returned. "I don't need pity. I'm content with my life, just as it is. I had a rough time. So what? Plenty of people do. I'm here to talk about a case, Jessica, and it isn't mine."

She smiled self-consciously. "All right, McCallum," she said agreeably, reaching for a file. "The baby was taken to Whitehorn Memorial and checked over. She's perfectly healthy, clean and well-cared for, barely two weeks old. They're keeping her for observation overnight and then it will be up to the juvenile authorities to make arrangements about her care until her parents are located. I'm going over to see her in the morning. I'd like you to come with me."

"I don't need to see it—"

"*Her,*" she corrected. "Baby Jennifer."

"—to start searching for its parents," he concluded without missing a beat.

"Her parents," Jessica corrected calmly.

His dark eyes didn't blink. "Was there anything else?"

"I'll leave here about nine," Jessica continued. "You can ride with me."

His eyes widened. "In that glorified yellow tank you drive?"

"It's a pickup truck!" she exclaimed defensively. "And it's very necessary, considering where I live!"

He refused to think about her cabin in the middle of nowhere, across a creek that flooded with every cloudburst. It wasn't his place to worry about her just because she had no family. In that aspect of their lives they were very much alike. In other ways…

He stood up. "You can ride with me," he said, giving in with noticeable impatience.

"I hate riding around in a patrol car," she muttered.

"It doesn't have a sign on it. It's a plainclothes car."

"Of course it is, with those plain hubcaps, no white sidewalls, fifteen antennas sticking out of it and a spotlight. It doesn't need a sign, does it? Anyone who isn't blind would recognize it as an unmarked patrol car!"

"It beats driving a yellow tank," he pointed out.

She stood up, too, feeling at a disadvantage when she didn't. But he was still much taller than she was. She pushed at a wisp of brown hair that had escaped from the bun on top of her head. Her beige suit emphasized her slender build, devoid as it was of any really noticeable curves.

"Why do you screw your hair up like that?" he asked curiously.

"It falls in my face when I'm trying to work," she said, indicating the stack of files on her desk. "Besides Candy,

I only have two caseworkers, and they're trying to take away one of them because of new budget cuts. I'm already working Saturdays trying to catch up, and they've just complained about the amount of overtime I do."

"That sounds familiar."

"I know," she said cheerily. "Everyone has to work around tight budgets these days. It's one of the joys of public service."

"Why don't you get married and let some strong man support you?" he taunted.

She tilted her chin saucily. "Are you proposing to me, Deputy?" she asked with a wicked smile. "Has someone been tantalizing you with stories of my homemade bread?"

He'd meant it sarcastically, but she'd turned the tables on him neatly. He gave in with a reluctant grin.

"I'm not the marrying kind," he said. "I don't want a wife and kids."

Her bright expression dimmed a little, but remnants of the smile lingered. "Not everyone does," she said agreeably. The loud interruption of the telephone ringing in the outer office caught her attention, followed by the insistent buzz of the intercom. She turned back to her desk. "Thanks for stopping by. I'll see you in the morning, then," she added as she lifted the receiver. "Yes, Candy," she said.

McCallum's eyes slid quietly over her bowed head. After a minute, he turned and walked out, closing the door gently behind him. He did it without a goodbye. Early in his life, he'd learned not to look back.

* * *

The house where McCallum lived was at the end of a wide, dead-end street. His neighbors never intruded, but it got back to him that they felt more secure having a law-enforcement officer in the neighborhood. He sat on his front porch sometimes with a beer and looked at the beauty of his surroundings while watching the children ride by on bicycles. He watched as a stranger watches, learning which children belonged at which houses. He saw affection from some parents and amazing indifference from others. He saw sadness and joy. But he saw it from a distance. His own life held no highs or lows. He was answerable to no one, free to do whatever he pleased with no interference.

He'd had the flu last winter. He'd lain in his bed for over twenty-four hours, burning with fever, unable to cook or even get into the kitchen. Not until he missed work did anyone come looking for him. The incident had punctuated how alone he really was.

He hadn't been alone long. Jessica had hotfooted it over to look after him, ignoring his ranting and raving about not wanting any woman cluttering up his house. She'd fed him and cleaned for him in between doing her own job, and only left when he proved to her that he could get out of bed. Because of the experience, he'd been ruder than ever to her. When he'd gone back to work, she'd taken a pot of chicken soup to the office, enough that he could share it with the other men on his shift. It had been uncomfortable when they'd teased him about Jessica's nurturing, and he'd taken out that irritation on her.

He hadn't even thanked her for her trouble, he recalled. No matter how rude he was she kept coming back, like a friendly little elf who only wanted to make him happy. She was his one soft spot, although, thank God, she didn't know it. He was curt with her because he had to keep her from knowing about his weakness for her. He had been doing a good job; when she looked at him these days, she never met his eyes.

He sipped his beer, glowering at the memories. His free hand dropped to the head of his big brown-and-black Doberman. He'd had the dog for almost a year. He'd found Mack tied in a croker sack, yipping helplessly in the shallows of a nearby river. Having rescued the dog, he couldn't find anyone who was willing to take it, and he hadn't had the heart to shoot it. There was no agency in Whitehorn to care for abandoned or stray animals. The only alternative was to adopt the pup, and he had.

At first Mack had been a trial to him. But once he housebroke the dog and it began to follow him around the house—and later, to work—he grew reluctantly fond of it. Now Mack was part of his life. They were inseparable, especially on hunting and fishing trips. If he had a family at all, McCallum thought, it was Mack.

He sat back, just enjoying the beauty of Whitehorn. The sun set; the children went inside. And still McCallum sat, thinking and listening to the hum of the quiet spring-time night.

Finally, he got up. It was after eleven. He'd just gone inside and was turning out the lights when the phone rang.

"It's Hensley," the sheriff announced over the phone. "We've got a 10-16 at the Miles place, a real hummer. It's outside the city police's jurisdiction, so it either has to be you or a deputy."

"It won't do any good to go, you know," McCallum said. "Jerry Miles beats Ellen up twice a month, but she never presses charges. Last time he beat up their twelve-year-old son, and even then—"

"I know."

"I'll go anyway," McCallum said. "It's a hell of a shame we can't lock him up without her having to press charges. She's afraid of him. If she left him, he'd probably go after her, and God knows what he'd do. I've seen it happen. So have you. Everybody says leave him. Nobody says they'll take care of her when he comes looking for her with a gun."

"We have to keep hoping that she'll get help."

"Jessica has tried," McCallum admitted, "but nothing changes. You can't help people until they're ready to accept it, and the consequences of accepting it."

"I heard that."

McCallum drove out to the Miles home. It was three miles out of Whitehorn, in the rolling, wide-open countryside.

He didn't put on the siren. He drove up into the yard and cut the lights. Then he got out, unfastening the loop that held his pistol in place in the holster on his hip, just in case. One of Whitehorn's policemen had been shot and killed trying to break up a domestic dispute some years ago.

There was no noise coming from inside. The night was ominously quiet. McCallum's keen eyes scanned the area and suddenly noticed a yellow truck parked just behind the house, on a dirt road that ran behind it and parallel to the main highway.

Jessica was in there!

He quickened his steps, went up on the front porch and knocked at the door.

"Police," he announced. "Open up!"

There was a pause. His hand went to the pistol and he stood just to the side of the doorway, waiting.

The main door opened quite suddenly, and a tired-looking Jessica Larson smiled at him through a torn screen. "It's all right," she said, opening the screen door for him. "He's passed out on the bed. Ellen and Chad are all right."

McCallum walked into the living room, feeling uncomfortable as he looked at the two people whose lives were as much in ruin as the broken, cheap lamp on the floor. The sofa was stained and the rug on the wood floor had frayed edges. There were old, faded curtains at the windows and a small television still blaring out a game show. Ellen sat on the sofa with red-rimmed eyes, her arm around Chad, who was crying. He had a bruise on one cheek.

"How much longer are you going to let the boy suffer like this, Ellen?" McCallum asked quietly.

She stared at him from dull eyes. "Mister, if I send my husband to jail, he says he'll kill me," she announced. "I think he will. Last time I tried to run away, he shot our dog."

"He's sick, Ellen," Jessica added gently. Her glance in the direction of the bedroom had an odd, frightened edge to it. "He's very sick. Alcoholism can destroy his body, you know. It can kill him."

"Yes, ma'am, I know that. He's a big man, though," the woman continued in a lackluster voice, absently smoothing her son's hair. "He loves me. He says so. He's always sorry, after."

"He's not sorry," McCallum said, his voice deep and steady. "He enjoys watching you cry. He likes making you afraid of him. He gets off on it."

"McCallum!" Jessica said sharply.

He ignored her. He knelt in front of Ellen and stared at her levelly. "Listen to me. My mother was an alcoholic. She used a bottle on me once, and laughed when she broke my arm with it. She said she was sorry, too, after she sobered up, but the day she broke my arm, I stopped believing it. I called the police and they locked her up. And the beatings stopped. For good."

Ellen wiped at her eyes. "Weren't you sorry? I mean, she was your mother. You're supposed to love your mother."

"You don't beat the hell out of people you love," he said coldly. "And you know that. Are you going to keep making excuses for him until he kills your son?"

She gasped, clasping the boy close. "But he won't!" she said huskily. "Oh, no, I know he won't! He loves Chad. He loves me, too. He just drinks so much that he forgets he loves us, that's all."

"If he hurts the child, you'll go to jail as an accessory," McCallum told her. He said it without feeling, without remorse. He said it deliberately. "I swear to God you will. I'll arrest you myself."

Ellen paled. The hands holding her son contracted. "Chad doesn't want to see his daddy go to jail," she said firmly. "Do you, Son?"

Chad lifted his head from her shoulder and looked straight at McCallum. "Yes, sir, I do," he said in a choked voice. "I don't want him to hit my mama anymore. I tried to stop him and he did this." He pointed to his eye.

McCallum looked back at Ellen. There was accusation and cold anger in his dark eyes. They seemed to see right through her.

She shivered. "He'll hurt us if I let you take him to jail," she said, admitting the truth at last. "I'm scared of him. I'm so scared!"

Jessica stepped forward. "There's a shelter for battered women," she replied. "I'll make sure you get there. You'll be protected. He won't come after you or Chad, and even if he tries, he can be arrested for that, too."

Ellen bit her lower lip. "He's my *husband*," she said with emphasis. "The good book says that when you take a vow, you don't ever break it."

McCallum's chin lifted. "The same book says that when a man marries a woman, he cherishes her. It doesn't say one damned thing about being permitted to beat her, does it?"

She hesitated, but only for a minute. "I have an aunt in Lexington, Kentucky. She'd let me and Chad live with her, I know she would. I could go there. He doesn't know about my aunt. He'd never find us."

"Is that what you want?" Jessica asked.

The woman hesitated. Her weary eyes glanced around the room, taking measure of the destruction. She felt as abused as the broken lamp, as the sagging sofa with its torn fabric. Her gaze rested finally on her son and she looked, really looked, at him. No child of twelve should have eyes like that. She'd been thinking only of her own safety, of her vows to her husband, not of the one person whose future should have mattered to her. She touched Chad's hair gently.

"It's all right, Son," she said. "It's gonna be all right. I'll get you out of here." She glanced away from his wet eyes to McCallum. Her head jerked toward the bedroom. "I have to get away. I can't press charges against him...."

"Don't worry about it," McCallum said. "He'll sleep for a long time and then he won't know where to look for you. By the time he thinks about trying, he'll be drunk again. The minute he gets behind a wheel, I'll have him before a judge. With three prior DWI convictions, he'll spend some time in jail."

"All right." She got uneasily to her feet. "I'll have to get my things...." Her eyes darted nervously to the bedroom.

McCallum walked to the doorway and stood there. He didn't say a word, but she knew what his actions meant. If her husband woke up while she was packing, McCallum would deal with him.

She smiled gratefully and went hesitantly into the dimly lit bedroom, where her husband was passed out on the bed. Jessica didn't offer to go with her. She sat very still on the sofa, looking around her with a kind of subdued fear that piqued McCallum's curiosity.

Jessica drove her own truck to the bus station, parking it next to the unmarked car in which McCallum had put Chad and his mother. It was acting up again, and she tried to recrank it but it refused to start.

They saw the mother and son onto the bus and stood together until it vanished into the distance.

McCallum glanced at his watch. It was after midnight, but he was wound up and not at all sleepy.

Jessica mistook the obvious gesture for an indication that he wanted to get going. "Thanks for your help," she told him. "I'd better get back home. Could you take me? My truck's on the blink again."

"Sure. I'll send someone over in the morning to fix the truck and deliver it to your office. I'm sure you can get a ride to work."

"Yes, I can. Thanks," she said, relieved.

He caught her arm and shepherded her into the depot, which was open all night. There was a small coffee concession, where an old man sold coffee and doughnuts and soft drinks.

Jessica was dumbfounded. Usually McCallum couldn't wait to get away from her. His wanting to have coffee with her was an historic occasion, and she didn't quite know what to expect.

Two

McCallum helped her into a small booth and came back with two mugs of steaming coffee.

"What if I didn't drink coffee?" she asked.

He smiled faintly. "I've never seen you without a cup at your elbow," he remarked. "No cream, either. Sugar?"

She shook her head. "I live on the caffeine, not the taste." She cupped her hands around the hot cup and looked at him across the table. "You don't like my company enough to take me out for coffee unless you want something. What is it?"

He was shocked. Did she really have such a low self-image? His dark eyes narrowed on her face, and he couldn't decide why she looked so different. She wasn't wearing makeup—probably she'd been in too big a hurry to get to Ellen's house to bother. And her infrequently worn, big-lensed glasses were perched jauntily on her nose. But it was more than that. Then he realized what the difference was. Her hair—her long, glorious, sable-colored hair—was falling in thick waves around her shoulders and halfway down her back. His fingers itched to bury themselves in it, and the very idea made his eyebrows fly up in surprise.

"I don't read minds," she said politely.

"What?" He frowned, then remembered her question. "I wanted to ask you something."

She nodded resignedly and sipped at her coffee.

He leaned back against the dark red vinyl of the booth, studying her oval face and her big brown eyes behind the round lenses for longer than he meant to. "How is it you wound up in that house during a domestic dispute?"

"Oh. That."

He glared at her. "Don't make light of it," he said shortly. "More cops have been hurt during family quarrels than in shoot-outs."

"Yes, I know, I do read statistics. Ellen called me and I went. That's all."

One eye narrowed. "Next time," he said slowly, "you phone me first, before you walk into something like that. Do you understand me?"

"But I was in no danger," she began.

"The man weighs two-fifty if he weighs a pound," he

said shortly. "You're what—a hundred and twenty sopping wet?"

"I'm not helpless!" She laughed nervously. It wouldn't do to let him know the terror she'd felt when Ellen had called her, crying hysterically, begging her to come. It had taken all her courage to walk into that house.

"Do you have martial-arts training?"

She hesitated and then shook her head irritably.

"Do you carry a piece?"

"What would I do with a loaded gun?" she exclaimed. "I'd shoot my leg off!"

The scowl got worse. "Then how did you expect to handle a drunken man who outweighs you by over a hundred pounds and was bent on proving his strength to anyone who came within swinging range?"

She nibbled her lower lip and stared into her coffee. "Because Ellen begged me to. It's my job."

"No, it's not," he said firmly. "Your job is to help people who are down on their luck and to rescue kids from abusive environments. It doesn't include trying to do a policeman's work."

His eyes were unblinking. He had a stare that made her want to back up two steps. She imagined it worked very well on lawbreakers.

She let out a weary breath. "Okay," she said, holding up a slender, ringless hand. "I let my emotions get the best of me. I did something stupid and, fortunately, I didn't get hurt."

"Big of you to admit it," he drawled.

"You're a pain, McCallum," she told him bluntly.

"Funny you should mention it," he replied. "I made the same complaint about you to Hensley only this morning."

"Oh, I know you don't approve of me," she agreed. "You think social workers should be like you—all-business, treating people as though they were statistics, not getting emotionally involved—"

"Bingo!" he said immediately.

She put her coffee cup down gently. "A hundred years ago, most of the country south of here belonged to the Crow," she said, looking pointedly at him, because she knew about his ancestry. "They had a social system that was one of the most efficient ever devised. No one valued personal property above the needs of the group. Gifts were given annually among the whole tribe. When a man killed a deer, regardless of his own need, the meat was given away. To claim it for himself was unthinkable. Arguments were settled by gift giving. Each person cared about every other person in the village, and people were accepted for what they were. And no one was so solitary that he or she didn't belong, in some way, to every family."

He leaned forward. "With the pointed exception of Crazy Horse, who kept to himself almost exclusively."

She nodded. "With his exception."

"Someone told you that I had a Crow ancestor," he guessed accurately.

She shrugged. "In Whitehorn, everyone knows everyone else's business. Well, mostly, anyway," she added, because she was pretty sure that he didn't know about her own emotional scars. The incident had been hushed up because of the nature of the crime, and because there'd been a minor involved. It was just as well. Jessica couldn't have a permanent relationship with a man, even if she would have given most of a leg to have one with McCallum. He was perfect for her in every way.

"I'm more French Canadian in my ancestry than Crow." He studied her own face with quiet curiosity. She had a pretty mouth, like a little bow, and her nose was straight. Her big, dark eyes with their long, curly lashes were her finest feature. Even glasses didn't disguise their beauty.

"Are you nearsighted or farsighted?" he asked abruptly.

"Nearsighted." She adjusted her glasses self-consciously. "I usually wear contacts, but my eyes itch lately from all the grass cuttings. I'm blind as a bat without these. I couldn't even cross a street if I lost them."

His eyes fell to her hands. They were slightly tanned, long-fingered, with oval nails. Very pretty.

"Are you going to arrest Ellen's husband?" she asked suddenly.

He pursed his lips. "Now what do you think?"

"We didn't get Ellen to press charges," she reminded him.

"We couldn't have. If she had, she'd have to come

back and face him in court. She's afraid that he might kill her. He's threatened to," he reminded her. "But as it is, he won't know where to look for her, and even if he did, it won't matter."

"What do you mean?" she asked curiously.

His eyes took on a faint glitter, like a stormy night sky. "He gets drunk every night. He's got three previous convictions on DWI and he likes to mix it up in taverns. He'll step over the line and I'll have him behind bars, without Ellen's help. This time I'll make sure the charges stick. Drunkenness is no excuse for brutality."

She was remembering what he'd said to Ellen about his own mother breaking his arm with a bottle when he was a little boy.

She reached out without thinking and gently touched the long sleeve of his blue-patterned Western shirt. "Which arm was it?" she asked quietly.

The compassion in her voice hurt him. He'd never known it in his youth. Even now, he wasn't used to people caring about him in any way. Jessica did, and he didn't want her to. He didn't trust anyone close to him. Years of abuse had made him suspicious of any overture, no matter how well meant.

He jerked his arm away. "What you heard wasn't something you were meant to hear," he said icily. "You had no business being in the house in the first place."

She cupped her mug in her hands and smiled. The

words didn't sting her. She'd learned long ago not to take verbal abuse personally. Most children who'd been hurt reacted that way to kindness. They couldn't trust anymore, because the people they loved most had betrayed them in one way or another. His was the same story she'd heard a hundred times before. It never got easier to listen to.

But there was a big difference between anger and hostility. Anger was normal, healthy. Hostility was more habit than anything else, and it stemmed from low esteem, feelings of inadequacy. It was impersonal, unlike aggression, which was intended to hurt. A good social worker quickly learned the difference, and how not to take verbal outpourings seriously. McCallum was something of a psychologist himself. He probably understood himself very well by now.

"I didn't mean to snap," he said curtly.

She only smiled at him, her eyes warm and gentle. "I know. I've spent the past three years working with abused children."

He cursed under his breath. He was overly defensive with her because she knew too much about people like him, and it made him feel naked. He knew that he must hurt her sometimes with his roughness, but damn it, she never fought back or made sarcastic comments. She just sat there with that serene expression on her face. He wondered if she ever gave way to blazing temper or passion. Both were part and parcel of his tempestuous nature, although he usually managed to control them. Years of self-discipline had helped.

"You don't like being touched, do you?" she asked suddenly.

"Don't presume, ever, to psychoanalyze me," he replied bluntly. "I'm not one of your clients."

"Wasn't there any social worker who tried to help you?" she asked.

"They helped me," he retorted. "I had homes. Several of them, in fact, mostly on ranches."

Her hands tightened on the cup. "Weren't you loved?"

His eyes flashed like glowing coals. "If you mean have I had women, yes," he said with deliberate cruelty. "Plenty of them!"

Jessica surrendered the field. She should have known better than to pry. She didn't want to hear anything about his intimate conquests. The thought of him…like that…was too disturbing. She finished her coffee and dragged a dollar bill out of her pocket to pay for it.

"I'll take care of it," he said carelessly.

She looked at him. "No, you won't," she said quietly. "I pay my own way. Always."

She got up and paid the old man behind the counter, and walked out of the concession ahead of McCallum.

She was already unlocking her pickup truck when he got outside. Even if it wouldn't start, she needed her sweater. She got it out and locked it up again.

"You actually lock that thing?" he asked sarcastically. "My God, anyone who stole it would be doing you a favor."

"I can't afford theft insurance," she said simply. "Keeping my family home takes all my spare cash."

He remembered where she lived, across the creek on the outskirts of town, with a huge tract of land—hundreds of acres. She played at raising cattle on it, and she had a hired hand who looked after things for her. Jessica loved cattle, although she knew nothing about raising them. But prices were down and it wasn't easy. He knew that she was fighting a losing battle, trying to keep the place.

"Why not just sell out and move into one of the new apartment complexes?"

She turned and looked up at him. He was taller up close. "Why, because it's my home. My heritage," she said. "It was one of the first homes built in Whitehorn, over a hundred years ago. I can't sell it."

"Heritage is right here," he said abruptly, placing his hand against her shoulder and collarbone, in the general area of her heart.

The contact shocked her. She moved back, but the truck was in the way.

He smiled quizzically. "What are you so nervous about?" he asked lazily. "This isn't intimate."

She was flushed. The dark eyes that looked up into his were a little frightened.

He stared at her until images began to suggest themselves, and still he didn't move his hand. "You've had to go a lot of places alone, to interview people who wanted assistance," he began. "At least one or two of those places must have had men very much like Ellen's husband—men who were drunk or who thought that a woman coming into a house alone must be asking for it. And when you were younger, you wouldn't have expected…" She caught her breath and his chin lifted. "Yes," he said slowly, almost to himself. "That's it. That's why you're so jumpy around men. I noticed it at Ellen's house. You were concerned for her, but that wasn't altogether why you kept staring so nervously toward the bedroom."

She bit her lower lip and looked at his chest instead of his eyes. His pearl-button shirt was open down past his collarbone, and she could see a thick, black mat of curling hair inside. He was the most aggressively masculine man she'd ever known, and God only knew why she wasn't afraid of him when most men frightened her.

"You won't talk, will you?" he asked above her head.

"McCallum…" She caught his big hand, feeling its strength and warmth. She told herself to push it away, but her fingers couldn't seem to do what her brain was telling them.

His breathing changed, suddenly and audibly. His warm breath stirred the hair at her temple. "But despite whatever happened to you," he continued as if she hadn't spoken, "you're not afraid of me."

"You must let me go now." She spoke quietly. Her hand went flat against his shirtfront. She knew at once that it was a mistake when she felt the warm strength of his body and the cushy softness of the thick hair under the shirt. The feel of him shocked her. "My... goodness, you're—you're furry," she said with a nervous laugh.

"Furry." He deliberately unsnapped two pearly buttons and drew the fabric from under her flattened hand. He guided her cold fingers over the thick pelt that covered him from his collarbone down, and pressed them over the hard nipple.

She opened her mouth to protest, but his body fascinated her. She'd never seen a man like this at close range, much less touched one. He smelled of soap and faint cologne. He drowned her in images, in sensations, in smells. Her fascinated eyes widened as she gave way to her curiosity and began to stroke him hesitantly.

He shivered. Her gaze shot up to his hard face, but his expression was unreadable—except for the faint, unnerving glitter of his eyes.

"A man's nipple is as sensitive as a woman's," he explained quietly. "It excites me when you trace it like that."

The soft words brought her abruptly to her senses. She was making love to a man on a public street in front of the bus depot. With a soft groan, she dragged her hand away from him and bit her lower lip until she tasted blood.

"What a horrified expression," he murmured as he refastened his shirt. "Does it shock you that you can feel like a woman? Or don't you think I know that you hide your own emotions in the job? All this empathy you pour out on your clients is no more than a shield behind which you hide your own needs, your own desires."

Her face tightened. "Don't *you* psychoanalyze *me!*" she gasped, throwing his earlier words right back at him.

"If I'm locked up inside, so are you, honey," he drawled, watching her react to the blunt remark.

"My personal life is my own business, and don't you call me honey!"

She started to turn, but he caught her by the upper arms and turned her back around. His eyes were merciless, predatory.

"Were you raped?" he asked bluntly.

"No!" she said angrily, glaring at him. "And that's all you need to know, McCallum!"

His hands on her arms relaxed, became caressing. He scowled down at her, searching for the right words.

"Let me go!"

"No."

He reached around her and relocked the truck. He helped her into his car without asking if she was ready to come with him, started it and drove straight to his house.

She was numb with surprise. But she came out of her stupor when he pulled the car into his driveway and turned off the engine and lights. "Oh, I can't," she began quickly. "I have to go home!"

Ignoring her protest, he got out and opened the door for her. She let him extricate her and lead her up onto his porch. Mack barked from inside, but once Sterling let them in and turned on the lights, he calmed the big dog easily.

"You know Mack," he told Jessica. "While you're getting reacquainted, I'll make another pot of coffee. If you need to wash your face, bathroom's there," he added, gesturing toward a room between the living room and the kitchen.

Mack growled at Jessica. She would try becoming his friend later, but right now she wanted to bathe her hot face. She couldn't really imagine why she'd allowed McCallum to bring her here, when it was certainly going to destroy her reputation if anyone saw her alone with him after midnight.

By the time she got back to the living room, he had hot coffee on the coffee table, in fairly disreputable black mugs with faded emblems on them.

"I don't have china," he said when she tried to read the writing on hers.

"Neither do I," she confessed. "Except, I do have two place settings of Havilland, but it's cracked. It was my great-aunt's." She looked at him over her coffee cup. "I shouldn't be here."

"Because it's late and we're alone?"

She nodded.

"I'm a cop."

"Well...yes."

"Your reputation won't suffer," he said, leaning back to cross his long legs. "If there's one thing I'm not, it's a womanizer, and everyone knows it. I don't have women."

"You said you did," she muttered.

He looked toward her with wise, amused eyes. "*Did*, yes. Not since I came back here. Small towns are hotbeds of gossip, and I've been the subject of it enough in my life. I won't risk becoming a household word again just to satisfy an infrequent ache."

She drank her coffee quickly, trying to hide how much his words embarrassed her, as well as the reference to gossip. She had her own skeletons, about which he apparently knew nothing. It had been a long time ago, after all, and most of the people who knew about Jessica's past had moved away or died. Sheriff Judd Hensley knew, but he wasn't likely to volunteer information to McCallum. Judd was tight-lipped, and he'd been Jessica's foremost ally at a time when she'd needed one desperately.

After a minute, Sterling put down his coffee cup and took hers away from her, setting it neatly in line with his. He leaned back on the sofa, his body turned toward hers.

"Tell me."

She clasped her hands tightly in her lap. "I've never talked about it," she said shortly. "He's dead, anyway, so what good would it do now?"

"I want to know."

"Why?"

His broad shoulders rose and fell. "Who else is there? You don't have any family, Jessica, and I know for a fact you don't have even one friend. Who do you talk to?"

"I talk to God!"

He smiled. "Well, He's probably pretty busy right now, so why don't you tell me?"

She pushed back her long hair. Her eyes sought the framed print of a stag in an autumn forest on the opposite wall. "I can't."

"Have you told anyone?"

Her slender shoulders hunched forward and she dropped her face into her hands with a heavy sigh. "I told my supervisor. My parents were dead by then, and I was living alone."

"Come on," he coaxed. "I may not be your idea of the perfect confidant, but I'll never repeat a word of it. Talking is therapeutic, or so they tell me."

His tone was unexpectedly tender. She glanced at him, grimaced at the patience she saw there—as if he were willing to wait all night if he had to. She might as well tell him a little of what had happened, she supposed.

"I was twenty," she said. "Grass green and sheltered. I knew nothing about men. I was sent out as a case-worker to a house where a man had badly beaten his wife and little daughter. I was going to question his wife one more time after she suddenly withdrew the charges. I went there to find out why, but she wasn't at home and he blamed me for his having been accused. I'd encouraged his wife and daughter to report what happened. He hit me until I couldn't stand up, and then he stripped me...." She paused, then forced the rest of it out. "He didn't rape me, although I suppose he would have if his brother-in-law hadn't driven up. He was arrested and charged, but he plea-bargained his way to a reduced sentence."

"He wasn't charged with attempted rape?"

"One of the more powerful city councilmen was his brother," she told him. She left out the black torment of those weeks. "He was killed in a car wreck after being parolled, and the councilman moved away."

"So he got away with it," McCallum murmured angrily. He smoothed his hand over his hair and stared out the dark window. "I thought you'd led a sheltered, pampered life."

"I did. Up to a point. My best friend had parents who drank too much. There were never any charges, and she hid her bruises really well. She's the reason I went into social work." She smiled bitterly. "It's amazing how much damage liquor does in our society, isn't it?"

He couldn't deny that. "Does your friend live here?"

She shook her head. "She lives in England with her husband. We lost touch years ago."

"Why in God's name didn't you give up your job when you were attacked?"

"Because I do a lot of good," she replied quietly.

"After it happened, I thought about quitting. It was only when the man's wife came to me and apologized for what he'd done, and thanked me for trying to help, that I realized I had at least accomplished something. She took her daughter and went to live with her mother.

"I cared too much about the children to quit. I still do. It taught me a lesson. Now, when I send caseworkers out, I always send them in pairs, even if it takes more time to work cases. Some children have no advocates except us."

"God knows, someone needs to care about them," he replied quietly. "Kids get a rough shake in this world."

She nodded and finished her coffee. Her eyes were curious, roaming around the room. There were hunting prints on the walls, but no photographs, no mementos. Everything that was personal had something military or work-related stamped on it. Like the mugs with the police insignias.

"What are you looking for? Sentiment?" he chided. "You won't find it here. I'm not a sentimental man."

"You're a caring one, in your way," she returned. "You were kind to Ellen and Chad."

"Taking care of emotionally wounded people goes with the job," he reminded her. He picked up his coffee cup and sipped the black liquid. His dark eyes searched hers. "I'll remind you again that I don't need hero worship from a social worker with a stunted libido."

"Why, McCallum, I didn't know you knew such big

words," she murmured demurely. "Do you read diction-
aries in your spare time? I thought you spent it polishing your pistol."

He chuckled with reserved pleasure. His deep voice
sounded different when he laughed, probably because
the sound was so rare, she mused.

"What do you do with yours?" he asked.

"I do housework," she said. "And read over case files.
I can't sit around and do nothing. I have to stay busy."

He finished his coffee and got up. "Want another
cup?" he asked.

She shook her head and stood up, too. "I have to get
home. Tomorrow's another workday."

"Let me open the latch for Mack so that he has access
to the backyard and I'll take you over there."

"Won't he run off?" she asked.

"He's got a fenced-in area and his own entrance," he
replied. "I keep it latched to make sure the neighbor's
damned cat stays out of the house. It walks in and helps
itself to his dog food when I'm not home. It climbs
right over the fence!"

Jessica had to smother a laugh, he sounded so dis-
gusted. She moved toward the dog, who suddenly
growled up at her.

She stopped dead. He was a big dog, and pretty
menacing at close range.

"Sorry," McCallum said, tugging Mack toward his
exit in the door. "He's not used to women."

"He's big, isn't he?" she asked, avoiding any further comment.

"Big enough. He eats like a horse." He took his car keys out of his pocket and locked up behind her while she got into the car.

They drove back toward her place. The night sky was dark, but full of stars. The sky went on forever in this part of the country, and Jessica could understand how McCallum would return here. She herself could never really leave. Her heart would always yearn for home in Montana.

When they got to her cabin, there was a single lighted window, and her big tomcat was outlined in it.

"That's Meriwether," she told him. "He wandered up here a couple of years ago and I let him stay. He's an orange tabby with battle-scarred ears."

"I hate cats," he murmured as he stopped the car at her front door.

"That doesn't surprise me, McCallum. What surprises me is that you have a pet at all—and that you even allow a stray cat on your property."

"Sarcasm is not your style, Miss Larson," he chided.

"How do you know? Other than the time you were sick, you only see me at work."

He pursed his lips and smiled faintly. "It's safer that way. You lonely spinsters are dangerous."

"Not me. I intend to be a lonely spinster for life," she said firmly. "Marriage isn't in my plans."

He scowled. "Don't you want kids?"

She opened her purse and took out her house key. "I like my life exactly as it is. Thanks for the lift. And the shoulder." She glanced at him a little self-consciously.

"I'm a clam," he said. "I don't broadcast secrets; my own or anyone else's."

"That must be why you're still working for Judd Hensley. He's the same way."

"He knew about your problem, I gather?"

She nodded. "He's been sheriff here for a long time. He and his wife were good friends of my parents. I'm sorry about their divorce. He's a lonely man these days."

"Loneliness isn't a disease," he muttered. "Despite the fact that you women like to treat it like one."

"Still upset about my bringing you that pot of soup, aren't you?" she asked him. "Well, you were sick and nobody else was going to feed and look after you. I'm a social worker. I like taking care of the underprivileged."

"I am *not* underprivileged."

"You were sick and alone."

"I wouldn't have starved."

"You didn't have any food in the house," she countered. "What did you plan to do, eat your dog?"

He made a face. "Considering some of the things *he* eats, God forbid!"

"Well, I wouldn't eat Meriwether even if I really were starving."

He glanced at the cat in the window. "I don't blame you. Anything that ugly should be buried, not eaten."

She made a sound deep in her throat and opened the car door.

"Go ahead," he invited. "Tell me he's not ugly."

"I wouldn't give you the satisfaction of arguing," she said smugly. "Good night."

"Lock that door."

She glowered at him. "I'm twenty-five years old." She pointed at her head. "This works."

"No kidding!"

She made a dismissive gesture with her hand and walked up onto the porch. She didn't look back, even when he beeped the horn as he drove away.

Three

Jessica unlocked her front door and walked into the familiar confines of the big cabin. A long hall led to the kitchen, past a spare bedroom. The floor, heart of pine, was scattered with worn throw rugs. The living and dining areas were in one room at the front. At the end of the hall near the kitchen was an elegant old bathroom. The plumbing drove her crazy in the winters—which were almost unsurvivable in this house—and the summers were hotter than blazes. She had no air-conditioning and the heating system was unreliable. She had to supplement it with fireplaces and scattered kerosene heaters. Probably one day she'd burn the whole place down around her ears trying to keep warm, but except for the infrequent cold, she remained healthy. She dreamed of a house that was livable year-round.

A soft meow came from the parlor, and Meriwether came trotting out to greet her. The huge tabby was marmalade colored. He'd been a stray when she found him, a pitiful half-grown scrap of fur with fleas and a stubby tail. She'd cleaned him up and brought him in, and they'd been inseparable ever since. But he hated men. He was a particularly big cat, with sharp claws, and he had to be locked up when the infrequent repairman was called to the house. He spat and hissed at them, and he'd even attacked the man who read the water meter. Now the poor fellow wouldn't come into the yard unless he knew Meriwether was safely locked in the house.

"Well, hello," she said, smiling as he wrapped himself around her ankle. "Want to hear all about the time I had?"

He made a soft sound. She scooped him up under one arm and started up the staircase. "Let me tell you, I've had better nights."

Later, with Meriwether curled up beside her, his big head on her shoulder, she slept, but the old nightmare came back, resurrected probably by the violence she'd seen and heard. She woke in a cold sweat, crying out in the darkness. It was a relief to find herself safe, here in her own house. Meriwether opened his eyes and looked at her when she turned on the light.

"Never mind. Go back to sleep," she told him gently. "I think I'll just read for a while."

She picked up a favorite romance novel from her shelf and settled back to read it. She liked these old ones best, the ones that belonged to a different world and always delivered a happy ending. Soon she was caught up in the novel and reality thankfully vanished for a little while.

At nine o'clock sharp the next morning, McCallum showed up in Jessica's office. He was wearing beige jeans and a sports jacket over his short-sleeved shirt this morning. No tie. He seemed to hate them; at least, Jessica had yet to see him dressed in one.

She was wearing a gray suit with a loose jacket. Her hair was severely confined on top of her head and she had on just a light touch of makeup. Watching her gather her briefcase, McCallum thought absently that he much preferred the tired woman of the night before, with her glorious hair loose around her shoulders.

"We'll go in my car," he said when they reached the parking lot, putting his sunglasses over his eyes. They gave him an even more threatening demeanor.

"I have to go on to another appointment, so I'll take my truck, now that it's been fixed, thanks to you...."

He opened the passenger door of the patrol car and stood there without saying a word.

She hesitated for a minute, then let him help her into

the car. "Are you deliberately intimidating, or does it just come naturally?" she asked when they were on the way to the hospital.

"I spent years ordering noncoms around," he said easily. "Old habits are hard to break. Plays hell at work sometimes. I keep forgetting that Hensley outranks me."

That sounded like humor, but she'd had no sleep to speak of and she felt out of sorts. She clasped her briefcase closer, glancing out the window at the landscape. Montana was beautiful in spring. The area around Whitehorn was uncluttered, with rolling hills that ran forever to the horizon and that later in the year would be rich with grain crops. Occasional herds of cattle dotted the horizon. There were cottonwood and willow trees along the streams, but mostly the country was wide open. It was home. She loved it.

She especially loved Whitehorn. With its wide streets and multitude of trees, the town reminded her of Billings—which had quiet neighborhoods and a spread-out city center, with a refinery right within the city limits. The railroad cut through Billings, just as it did here in Whitehorn. It was necessary for transportation, because mining was big business in southern Montana.

The Whitehorn hospital was surrounded by cottonwood trees. Its grounds were nicely landscaped and there was a statue of Lewis and Clark out front. William Clark's autograph in stone at Pompey's Pillar, near

Hardin, Montana, still drew photographers. The Lewis and Clark expedition had come right through Whitehorn.

Jessica introduced herself and McCallum to the ward nurse, and they were taken to the nursery.

Baby Jennifer, or Jenny as she was called, was in a crib there. She looked very pretty, with big blue eyes and a tiny tuft of blond hair on top of her head. She looked up at her visitors without a change of expression, although her eyes were alert and intelligent.

Jessica looked at her hungrily. She put down her briefcase and with a questioning glance at the nurse, who nodded, she picked the baby up and held her close.

"Little angel," she whispered, smiling so sadly that the man at her side scowled. She touched the tiny hand and felt it curl around her finger. She blinked back tears. She would never have a baby. She would never know the joy of feeling it grow in her body, watching its birth, nourishing it at her breast....

She made a sound and McCallum moved between her and the nurse with magnificent carelessness. "I want to see any articles of clothing that were found on or with the child," he said courteously.

The nurse, diverted, produced a small bundle. He unfastened it. There was one blanket, a worn pink one—probably homemade, judging by the hand-sewn border—with no label. There was a tiny gown, a pretty lacy thing with a foreign label, the sort that might be found at a fancy garage sale. There were some hand-knitted booties and a bottle. The bottle was a common plastic one with nothing outstanding about it. He sighed angrily. No clues here.

"Oh, yes, there's one more thing, Detective," the nurse said suddenly. She produced a small brooch, a pink cameo. "This was attached to the gown. Odd, isn't it, to put something so valuable on a baby? This looks like real gold."

McCallum touched it, turned it over. It was gold, all right, and very old. That was someone's heirloom. It might be the very clue he needed to track down the baby's parents.

He fished out a plastic bag and dropped the cameo into it, fastening it and sticking it in his inside jacket pocket. It was too small to search for prints, and it had been handled by too many people to be of value in that respect. Hensley had checked all these things yesterday when the baby was found. The bottle had been wiped clean of prints, although not by anybody at the Kincaid home. Apparently the child's parents weren't anxious to be found. The puzzling thing was that brooch. Why wipe fingerprints off and then include a probably identifiable piece of heirloom jewelry?

He was still frowning when he turned back to Jessica. She was just putting the child into its crib and straightening. The look on her face was all too easy to read, but she quickly concealed her thoughts with a businesslike expression.

"We'll have to settle her with a child-care provider until the court determines placement," Jessica told the nurse. "I'll take care of that immediately when I get back to the office. I'll need to speak to the attending physician as well."

"Of course, Miss Larson. If you'll come with me?"

McCallum fell into step beside her, down the long hall to Dr. Henderson's office. They spoke with him about the child's condition and were satisfied that she could be released the next morning.

"I'll send over the necessary forms," Jessica assured him, shaking hands.

"Pity, isn't it?" the doctor said sadly. "Throwing away a baby, like a used paper plate."

"She wasn't exactly thrown away," Jessica reminded him. "At least she was left where people would find her. We've had babies who weren't so fortunate."

McCallum pursed his lips. "Has anyone called to check on the baby?" he asked suddenly.

"Why, yes," the doctor replied curiously. "As a matter of fact, a woman from *The Whitehorn Journal* office called. She wanted to do a story, but I said she must first check with you."

McCallum lifted an eyebrow. "*The Whitehorn Journal* doesn't have a woman reporter."

He frowned. "I understood her to say the *Journal*. I may have been mistaken."

"I doubt it," McCallum said thoughtfully. "It was

probably the child's mother, making sure the baby had been found."

"If she calls again, I'll get in touch with you."

"Thanks," McCallum said.

He and Jessica walked back down the hall toward the hospital exit. He glanced down at her. "How old are you?"

She started. "I'm twenty-five," she said. "Why?"

He looked ahead instead of at her, his hands stuck deep in his jean pockets. "These modern attitudes may work for some women, but they won't work for you. Why don't you get married and have babies of your own, instead of mooning over someone else's?"

She didn't answer him. Rage boiled up inside her, quickening her steps as she made her way out the door toward his car.

He held the door open for her. She didn't even bother to comment on the courtesy or question it, she was so angry. He had no right to make such remarks to her. Her private life was none of his business!

He got in beside her, but he didn't start the engine. He turned toward her, his keen eyes cutting into her face. "You cried," he said shortly.

She grasped her briefcase like a lifeline, staring straight ahead, ignoring him.

He hit the steering wheel with his hand in impotent anger. He shouldn't let her get to him this way.

"How can you be in law enforcement with a temper like that?" she demanded icily.

He stared at her levelly. "I don't hit people."

"You do, too!" she raged. "You hit that man who threatened to pull a gun on you. I heard all about it!"

"Did you hear that *he* kicked me in the... Well, never mind, but he damned near unmanned me before I laid a finger on him!" he said harshly.

She clutched the briefcase like a shield. "McCallum, you are crude! Crude and absolutely insensitive!"

"Crude? Insensitive?" he exclaimed shortly. He glared at her. "If you think that's crude, suppose I give you the slang term for it then?" he added with a cold smile, and he told her, graphically, what the man had done.

She was breathing through her nostrils. Her eyes were like brown coals, and she was livid.

"Your hand is itching, isn't it?" he taunted. "You want to slap me, but you can't quite work up the nerve."

"You have no right to talk to me like this!"

"How did you ever get into this line of work?" he demanded. "You're a bleeding-heart liberal with more pity than purpose in your life. If you'd take down that hair—" he pulled some pins from her bun "—and keep on those contact lenses, you might even find a man who'd marry you. Then you wouldn't have to spend your life burying your own needs in a job that's little more than a substitute for an adult relationship with a man!"

"You...!" The impact of the briefcase hitting his shoulder shocked him speechless. She hit him again before he could recover. The leather briefcase was heavy, but it was the shock of the attack that left him frozen in his seat when she tumbled out of the car and slammed the door furiously behind her.

She started off down the street with her hair hanging in unruly strands from its once-neat bun and her jacket askew. She looked dignified even in her pathetic state, and she didn't look back once.

Four

She made it two blocks before her feet gave out. Thank goodness for the Chamber of Commerce, she thought, taking advantage of the strategically placed bench near the curb bearing that agency's compliments. The late April sun was hot, and her suit, though light, was smothering her. The high heels she was wearing with it were killing her. She took off the right one, grimaced and rubbed her hose-clad foot.

She was suddenly aware of the unmarked patrol car that cruised to the curb and stopped.

McCallum got out without any rush and sat down beside her on the bench.

"You are the most difficult man I've ever met," she told him bluntly. "I don't understand why you feel compelled to make me so miserable, when all I've ever wanted to do was be kind to you!"

He leaned back, his eyes hidden behind dark sunglasses, and crossed his long legs. "I don't need kindness and I don't like your kind of woman."

"I know that," she said. "It shows. But I haven't done a thing to you."

He took off his sunglasses and turned his face toward her. It was as unreadable as stone, and about that warm. How could he tell her that her nurturing attitude made him want to scream? He needed a woman and she had a delectable body, but despite her response to him that night in front of the bus station, she backed away from him the minute he came too close. He wasn't conceited, yet he knew he was a physically dynamic, handsome man. Women usually ran after him, not the reverse. Jessica was the exception, and perhaps it was just as well. He wasn't a man with commitment on his mind.

"We're supposed to be working on a case together," he reminded her.

"I don't work on cases with men who talk to me as if I were a hooker," she shot back with cold dark eyes. "I don't have to take that sort of language from you. And I'll remind you that you're supposed to be upholding the law, not verbally breaking it. Or is using foul language in front of a woman no longer on the books as a misdemeanor in Whitehorn?"

He moved uncomfortably on the bench, because it *was* a misdemeanor. She'd knocked him off balance and he'd reacted like an idiot. He didn't like admitting it. "It wasn't foul language. It was explicit," he defended himself.

"Splitting hairs!"

"All right, I was out of line!" He shifted his long legs. "You get under my skin," he said irritably. "Haven't you noticed?"

"It's hard to miss," she conceded. "If I'm such a trial to you, Detective, there are other caseworkers in my office...."

He turned his head toward her. "Hensley said I work with you. So I work with you."

She reached down and put her shoe back on, unwittingly calling his attention to her long, elegant legs in silky hose.

"That doesn't mean we have to hang out together," she informed him. "We can talk over the phone when necessary."

"I don't like telephones."

Her eyes met his, exasperated. "Have you ever thought of making a list of your dislikes and just handing it to people?" she asked. "Better yet, you might consider a list of things you *do* like. It would be shorter."

He glowered at her. "I never planned to wind up being a hick cop in a hick town working with a woman who thinks a meaningful relationship has something to do with owning a cat."

"I can't imagine why you don't go back into the service, where you felt at home!"

"Made too many enemies." He bit off the words. "I don't fit in there, either, anymore. Everything's changing. New regulations, policies…"

"Did you ever think of becoming a diplomat?" she said with veiled sarcasm.

"No chance of that," he murmured heavily, then sighed. "I should have studied anthropology, I guess."

Her bad temper dissipated like clouds in sunlight. She could picture it. She laughed.

"Oh, hell, don't do that," he said shortly. "I didn't mean to be funny."

"I don't imagine so. Is your lack of diplomacy why you're not in the service anymore?"

He shook his head. "It didn't help my career. But the real problem was the new political climate. I'm no bigot, but I'm not politically correct when it comes to bending over backwards to please special-interest groups. If I don't like something, I can't pretend that I do. I didn't want to end up stationed in a microwavable room in Moscow, listening to people's conversations."

She frowned. "I thought you were in the navy? You know…sailing around in ships and stuff."

His dark eyes narrowed. "I didn't serve on a ship. I was in Naval Intelligence."

"Oh." She hadn't realized that. His past took on a whole new dimension in her eyes. "Then how in the world did you end up here?"

"I had to live someplace. I hate cities, and this is as close to a home as I've ever known," he said simply. "The last place I lived was with an elderly couple over near the county line. They're dead now, but they left me a little property in the Bighorn Mountains. Who knows, I may build a house there one day. Just for me and Mack."

"I don't think I like dogs."

"And I hate cats," he said at once.

"Why doesn't that surprise me?"

His eyebrow jumped. He put his sunglasses back on and got to his feet. He looked marvelously fit, all muscular strength and height, a man in the prime of his life. "I'll run you back to your office. I want to go out to the Kincaid place and have a talk with Jeremiah."

She stood up, holding her briefcase beside her. "I can walk. It's only another block or so."

"Five blocks, and it's midday," he reminded her. "Come on. I won't make any more questionable remarks."

"I'd like that sworn to," she muttered as she let him open the door for her.

"You're a hot-tempered little thing, aren't you?" he asked abruptly.

"I defend myself," she conceded. "I don't know about the 'little' part."

He got in beside her and started the engine. Five

minutes later she was back in the parking lot at her office. She was strangely reluctant to get out of the car, though. It was as though something had shifted between them, after weeks of working fairly comfortably with each other. He'd said 'the last place he lived,' and he'd mentioned an elderly couple, not parents.

"May I ask you something personal?" she said.

He looked straight at her, without removing his sunglasses. "No."

She was used to abruptness and even verbal abuse from clients, but McCallum set new records for it. He was the touchiest man she'd ever met.

"Okay," she said, clutching her briefcase as she opened the door. She looked over her shoulder. "Oh, I'm, uh, sorry about hitting you with this thing. I didn't hurt you, did I?"

"I've been shot a couple of times," he mentioned, just to make sure she got the idea that a bash with a briefcase wasn't going to do much damage.

"Poor old bullets," she muttered.

His face went clean of all expression, but his chest convulsed a time or two.

She got out of the car and slammed the door. She walked around to the driver's side and bent down. "I accept your apology."

"I didn't make any damned apology," he shot right back.

"I'm sure you meant to. I expect you were raised to be a gentleman, it's just that you've forgotten how."

The sunglasses glittered. She moved back a little.

"Don't you have anything to do? What the hell do they pay you for, and don't tell me it's for stand-up comedy."

"Actually, I'm doing a brain-surgery-by-mail course," she said pertly. "You're first on my list of potential patients."

"God forbid." He slipped the car into gear.

"Wait a minute," she said. "Are you going to tell anyone about the brooch you found?"

"No," he replied impatiently. "That brooch is my ace in the hole. I don't want it publicized in case someone comes to claim the baby. I'll mention it to selected people when it comes in useful."

"Oh, I see," she said at once. "You can rule out impostors. If they don't know about the brooch, they're not the baby's mother."

"Smart lady. Don't mention it to anyone."

"I wouldn't think of it. You'll let me know what you find out at the Kincaids', won't you?" she asked.

"Sure. But don't expect miracles. I don't think Dugin's the father, and I don't think we're going to find the baby's mother or any other relatives."

"The baby is blond," she said thoughtfully. "And so is Dugin."

"A lot of men in this community are blond. Besides, have you forgotten that Dugin is engaged to Mary Jo Plummer? With a dish like that wearing his ring, he isn't likely to be running around making other women pregnant."

"And he could afford to send it away if it was his, or have it adopted," she agreed. "Funny, though, isn't it, for someone to leave a baby on his doorstep? What did his father say?"

"Jeremiah wasn't there, according to Hensley. He'd been away and so Dugin called the law."

"That isn't like the Jeremiah Kincaid I know," she mused. "It would be more in character for him to start yelling his head off and accusing Dugin of fathering it."

"So I've heard."

He didn't say another word. Under that rough exterior, there had to be a heart somewhere. She kept thinking she might excavate it one day, but he was a hard case.

He gave her a curt nod, his mind already on the chore ahead. Dismissing her from his mind, he picked up the mike from his police radio and gave his position and his call letters and signed off. Without even a wave, he sped out of the parking lot.

She watched him until he was out of sight. She was feeling oddly vulnerable. There was a curious warm glow inside her as she went back into the office. She wished she understood her own reactions to the man. McCallum confused and delighted her. Of course, he also made her homicidal.

McCallum went out to the Kincaid ranch the next day, with the brooch in hand. He had some suspicions about that brooch, and it would be just as well to find out if anyone at the ranch recognized it.

When he drove up, the door was opened by Jeremiah himself. He was tall and silver haired, a handsome man in his late sixties. His son was nothing like him, in temperament or looks. Jeremiah had a face that a movie star would have envied.

"Come on in, McCallum, I've been expecting you," Jeremiah said cordially. "Can I pour you a whiskey?"

Characteristically, the man thought everyone shared his own fondness for Old Grandad. McCallum, when he drank, which was rarely, liked the smoothness of scotch whiskey.

"No, thanks. I'm working," McCallum replied.

"You cops." Jeremiah shook his head and poured himself a drink. "Now," he said, when they were seated on the elegant living room furniture, "how can I help you?"

McCallum pulled the brooch, in its plastic bag, out of his pocket and tossed it to the older man. Jeremiah stared at it for a long moment, one finger touching it lightly, reflectively. Then his head lifted.

"Nope," he told McCallum without any expression. "Never saw this before. If it was something that belonged to anyone in this family, you'd better believe I'd recognize it," he added.

He tossed it back to McCallum and lifted his glass to his lips. "What else can I tell you?"

"Was there anything on the baby that wasn't turned in when Sheriff Hensley came?" McCallum persisted.

"Not that I'm aware of," the other man said pleasantly. "Of course, I wasn't home at the time, you know. I didn't find out what had happened until the baby had been taken away. Hell of a thing, isn't it, for a mother to desert her child like that!"

"I didn't say it was deserted by its mother," McCallum replied slowly.

Jeremiah laughed, a little too loudly. "Well, it's hardly likely that the baby's father would have custody, is it? Even in these modern times, most men don't know what to do with a baby!"

"Apparently, some men still don't know how to prevent one, either."

Jeremiah grunted. "Maybe so." He glanced at the younger man. "It isn't Dugin's. I know there's been talk, but I asked the boy straight out. He said that since he got engaged to Mary Jo last year, there hasn't been any other woman."

"And you believe him?"

Jeremiah cleared his throat. "Dugin's sort of slow in that department. Takes a real woman to, uh, help him. That's why he's waited so late in life to marry. Mary Jo's a sweet little thing, but she's a firecracker, too. Caught her kissing him one afternoon out in the barn, and by God if they didn't almost go at it right there, standing up, in front of the whole world! She's something, isn't she, for a children's librarian."

McCallum's eyes were on the lean hands holding the glass of whiskey. They were restless, nervous. Jeremiah was edgy. He hid it well, but not with complete success.

"It sounds as though they'll have a good marriage."

"I think so. She's close to his age, and they sure enjoy being together. Pity about your boss's marriage," he added with a shrug, "but his wife always was too brainy for a man like that. I mean, after all, a cop isn't exactly an Ivy League boy." He noticed the look on McCallum's face and cleared his throat. "Sorry. No offense meant."

"None taken," Sterling replied. He got to his feet. "If you think of anything that might help us, don't hesitate to call."

"Sure, sure. Look, that crack I made about cops not having much education…"

"I took my baccalaureate degree in science while I was in the navy," he told Jeremiah evenly. "The last few years before I mustered out, I worked in Naval Intelligence."

Jeremiah was surprised. "With that sort of background, why are you working for the sheriff's department?"

"Maybe I just like small towns. And I did grow up here."

"But, man, you could starve on what you make in law enforcement!"

"Do you think so?" McCallum asked with a smile. "Thanks for your time, Mr. Kincaid."

He shook hands with the man and left, thinking privately that he'd rather work for peanuts in law enforcement than live the sort of aimless existence that Jeremiah Kincaid did. The man might have silver hair, but he was a playboy of the first order. He was hardly ever at home, and Dugin certainly wasn't up to the chore of taking care of a spread that size.

Speaking of Dugin… McCallum spotted him near the toolshed, talking to a younger man, and walked toward him.

Dugin shaded his eyes against the sun. He was tall and fair, in his forties, and he was mild-mannered and unassuming. He'd always seemed younger than he was. Perhaps it was because his father had always overshadowed him. Dugin still lived at home and did most everything his father told him to. He smiled and held out his hand when McCallum reached him.

"Nice day, isn't it?" Dugin asked. "What can I do for you, Deputy? And how's the kid?"

"She's fine. They're placing her in care until the case comes up. Listen, do you know anything that you haven't told the sheriff? Was there anything else with the baby that wasn't turned in?"

Dugin thought for a minute and shook his head. "Not a thing. It isn't my kid," he added solemnly. "I hear there's been some talk around Whitehorn about my being the father, but I'm telling you, I don't know anything. I wouldn't risk losing Mary Jo for any other woman, Deputy. Just between us," he added wryly, "I wouldn't have the energy."

McCallum chuckled. "Okay. Thanks."

"Keep in touch with us about the case, will you?" Dugin asked. "Even though it's not my child, I'd still like to know how things come out."

"Sure."

McCallum walked slowly back to his patrol car, wondering all the way why the baby had been left here, and with Dugin. There had to be a clue. He should have shown that cameo to Dugin, but if Jeremiah didn't recognize it, there was little point in showing it to his son. As Jeremiah had suggested, if it were a family heirloom, he would have recognized it immediately.

It was a lazy day, after that. McCallum was drinking coffee in the Hip Hop Café with his mind only vaguely on baby Jennifer and her missing parents. He was aware of faint interest from some of the other diners when his portable walkie-talkie made static as it picked up a call. Even though most people in White-horn knew him, he still drew some curiosity from tourists passing through. He was a good-looking man with a solid, muscular physique that wasn't overdone or exaggerated. He looked powerful, especially with the gun in its holster visible under his lightweight summer jacket.

The call that came over the radio made him scowl. He'd had enough of Jessica Larson the day before, but here she was after him again. Apparently there was a domestic disturbance at the Colson home, where a young boy lived with his father and grandmother.

Sterling went out to the car to answer the call, muttering all the way and as he sat down and jerked up the mike.

"Why is Miss Larson going?" he demanded.

"I don't know, K-236," the dispatcher drawled, using his call letters instead of his name. "And even if I did, I wouldn't tell you on an open channel."

"I'll see that you get a Christmas present for being such a good boy," McCallum drawled back.

There was an unidentified laugh as McCallum hung up and drove to the small cottagelike Colson house on a dirt road just out of town.

He got there before Jessica did. If there was a fight going on here, it wasn't anything obvious. Terrance Colson was sitting on the porch cleaning his rifle while his mother fed her chickens out back in the fenced-in compound. The boy, Keith, was nowhere in sight. Terrance was red-faced and seemed to have trouble holding the rifle still.

"Afternoon, McCallum!" Terrance called pleasantly. "What can I do for you?"

McCallum walked up on the porch, shook hands with the man and sat down on one of the chairs. "We had a report, but it must have been some crank," he said, looking around.

"Report of what?" Terrance asked curiously.

Before McCallum could answer, Jessica came driving up in her rickety yellow truck. She shut it off, but it kept running for a few seconds, knocking like crazy. That fan belt sounded as if it were still slipping, too. He'd noticed it the night at the bus station.

She got out, almost dropping her shoulder bag in the dirt, and approached the house. McCallum wondered just how many of those shapeless suits she owned. This one was green, and just as unnoticeable as the others. Her hair was up in a bun again. She looked the soul of business.

"Well, hello, Miss Larson," Terrance called. "We seem to be having a party today!"

She stopped at the steps and glanced around, frowning. "We had a call at the office…" she faltered for a moment "…about a terrible fight going on out here. I was requested to come and talk to you."

Terrance looked around pointedly, calling her attention to the peaceful surroundings. "What fight?"

She sighed. "An unnecessary call, I suppose," she said with a smile. "I'm sorry. But as I'm here already, do you think I might talk to Keith for a minute? He told his counselor at school that he'd like to talk to me when I had time."

Terrance stared at her without blinking. "Funny, he never said anything to me about it. And he's not here right now. He's out fishing."

"Do you think I could find him?" she asked persistently.

"He goes way back in the woods," he said quickly. "It's not a good time. He came home in a real bad mood. Best to leave him alone until he cools down."

She shrugged. "As you wish. But do tell him that I'll

be glad to listen any time he wants to talk about those school problems." She didn't add that she wondered why he couldn't tell them to the counselor, who was a good psychologist.

"I'll tell him," Terrance said curtly.

"Good day then." She smiled at Terrance, nodded at McCallum and went to climb back into her truck.

McCallum said his own goodbye, wondering why Mrs. Colson never came out of the chicken pen to say hello the whole time he was there. And Terrance's expression had hardened when he'd mentioned the boy. Odd.

He climbed into the patrol car and gave his call sign and location, announcing that he was back in service again. He followed after Jessica's sluggish truck and wondered if she was going to make it back into town.

When she parked her car at the office, he drove in behind her. The squealing of her fan belt was louder than ever. She really would have to do something about it when she had time.

"Your fan belt is loose," he told her firmly. "It's going to break one day and you'll be stranded."

"I know. I'm not totally stupid."

He got out of the car and walked with her to the office, not making a comment back, as he usually did. He seemed deep in thought. "Something funny's going on out at that place," he said suddenly. "Old Mrs. Colson hiding out with the chickens, Keith nowhere in sight, Terrance cleaning his gun, but without any gun oil...."

"You have a very suspicious mind," she accused gently. "For heaven's sake, do you always go looking for trouble? I'm delighted that there wasn't anything to it. I know the family, and they're good people. It's Keith who gives them fits. He's been into one bout of trouble after another at school since he was in the fifth grade. He's a junior now, and still getting into fights and breaking rules. He was picked up with another boy for shoplifting, although Keith swore he was innocent and the officers involved believed him. I've been trying to help the family as much as possible. Terrance lost his job at the manufacturing company that shut down last fall, and Milly is trying to make a little money by taking in ironing and doing alterations for the dry cleaners. The Colsons are hurting, but they're too proud to let me help much."

He frowned thoughtfully. "Isn't that the way of it?" he asked quietly. "The people who need help most never ask for it. On the other hand, plenty who don't deserve it get it."

She glowered up at him. "You're so cynical, McCallum! Don't you believe anybody can be basically good?"

"No."

She laughed and shook her head. "I give up. You're a hopeless case."

"I'm in law enforcement," he pointed out. "What we see doesn't lead us to look for the best in people."

"Neither does what I see, but I still try to believe in basic goodness," she replied.

He looked down at her for a long moment, letting his eyes linger on her soft mouth and straight nose before they lifted to catch her eyes.

"No, you don't," he said abruptly. "How can you still believe? What happens is that you just close your eyes to the ugliness. That's what most people do. They don't want to know that human beings can do such hideous things. Murder and robbery and beatings are so unthinkable that people pretend it can't occur. Then some terrible crime happens to them personally, and they have to believe it."

"You don't close your eyes to it," she said earnestly. "In fact, you look for it everywhere, even when you have to dig to find it. You have to try to rise above the ugliness."

His eyes darkened. He turned away. "I work for a living," he said lazily. "I haven't got time to stand around here socializing with you. Get that fan belt seen to."

She looked after him. "My goodness, do I really need a big, strong man to tell me how to take care of myself?"

"Yes."

He got into his car, leaving her aghast, and drove off.

Five

For several days, McCallum scoured the area for any clues as to the identity of the baby called Jennifer. He checked at every clinic and doctor's office in the area, as well as the local hospital and those in the surrounding counties. But every child's parents were accounted for. There were no leftover babies at any of the medical facilities. Which meant that the baby had probably been born at home, and a midwife had attended the birth. There were plenty of old women in the community who knew how to deliver a baby, and McCallum knew that he could spend years searching for the right person. Prospects looked dismal.

He was just leaving the office for lunch when Jessica Larson walked up to him on the street.

"I need to get your opinion on something," she said, and without preamble, caught his big, lean hand in hers and began to drag him off toward a parked car nearby.

"Now, hold it," he growled, hating and loving the feel of her soft hand in his.

"Don't grumble," she chided. "It won't hurt a bit. I just want you to talk to these young people for me before they make a big mistake." She paused at the beat-up old Chevy, where two teenagers sat guiltily in the front seat. They didn't look old enough to be out of school.

"This is Deputy McCallum," Jessica told the teens. "Ben and Amy want to get married," she explained to him. "Their parents are against it. Ben is seventeen and Amy is sixteen. I've told them that any marriage they make can be legally annulled by her parents because she's under age. Will you tell them that, too?"

He wasn't sure about the statutes on marriageable age in Montana, having never had occasion or reason to look them up. But he was pretty sure the girl was under the age of consent, and he knew what Jessica wanted him to say. He could bluff when he had to.

"She's absolutely right," he told them. "A minor can't legally marry without written permission from a parent. It would be terrible for you to have to—"

"She's pregnant," Ben mumbled, red-faced, and looked away. "I tried to get her to have it… Well, to not have it, really. She won't listen. She says we have to get married or her folks'll kill her."

Jessica hadn't counted on that complication. She stood there, stunned.

McCallum squatted down beside the car and looked at Amy, who was obviously upset. "Why don't we start at the beginning?" he asked her gently. "These are big decisions that need thought."

While Jessica looked on, stunned by the tenderness in McCallum's deep voice, Amy began to warm to him. "I don't know if I'm pregnant, really," she confessed slowly. "I think I am."

"Shouldn't you find out for sure, before you wind up in a marriage neither of you is ready for?" he asked evenly.

"Yes, sir."

"Then the obvious next step is to see a doctor, isn't it?"

She grimaced. "My dad'll kill me."

"I'll speak to your parents," Jessica promised her. "They won't kill you. They're good people, and they love you. You're their only child."

"I'd just love to have a baby," Amy said dreamily, looking at Ben with fantasy-filled eyes that didn't even see his desperation, his fear. "We can have a house of our own, and I can get a job…."

McCallum looked hard at Jessica.

"Let's go over to your parents' house, Amy," she said. She had McCallum firmly by the hand again, and she wasn't about to let go. "I'm sure Deputy McCallum won't mind coming with us," she added, daring him to say no.

He gave up plans for a hamburger and fries and told

his stomach to shut up. Resignedly, he helped Jessica into his car, and they followed the teens to Amy's house.

"It wasn't so bad, was it?" Jessica commented after the ordeal was finally over. "She'll see a doctor and then get counseling if she needs it. And there won't be a rushed marriage with no hope of success. They didn't even blame Ben too much."

"Why should they?" he muttered as he negotiated a right turn. "She's the one with dreams of babies and happy ever after, not him. He just wants to finish high school and go on to veterinary college."

"Ah, the man's eternal argument. 'Eve tempted me with the apple.'"

He glanced at her musingly. "Most women can lead a man straight to bed with very little conscious effort. Especially a young man."

She lifted her eyebrows. "Don't look at me. I've never led anyone to my bed with conscious effort or without it." She stemmed the memories that thoughts of intimacy resurrected.

"Have you wanted to?"

The question, coming from such an impersonal sort of man, surprised her. "Why…no."

"Have you let the opportunity present itself?" he persisted.

She straightened her skirt unnecessarily. "I'm sorry I made you miss your lunch."

He let the subject go. "How do you know you did?"

"Oh, you always go to lunch at eleven-thirty," she remarked. "I see you crossing over to the café from my office."

He chuckled softly, and it wasn't until she saw the speculation on his face that she realized why.

"I wasn't…watching you, for God's sake!" she blurted out, reddening.

"Really?" he teased. "You mean I've mistaken that hero worship in your eyes all this time?"

Her dark eyes glared at him. "You are very conceited."

"Made so by a very expressive young face," he countered. He glanced at her while they paused at a stop sign. "Don't build a pedestal under me, Jessie," he said, using a nickname for her for the first time. "I'm not tame enough for a woman like you."

She gaped at him. "If you think that I…!"

Incredibly, he caught the back of her head with a steely hand and leaned over her with slow, quiet intent. His dark eyes fell to her shocked mouth and he tugged gently until her mouth was a fraction below his. She could taste his minty breath, feel the heat of his mouth threatening her lips. She could feel the restrained passion in his long, fit body as it loomed over to hers.

"You're afraid of me," he whispered into her mouth. "And it has nothing to do with that bad experience you had. It isn't the kind of fear that causes nightmares. It's the kind that makes your body swell hard with desire."

While she was absorbing the muted shock the words produced, his mouth lowered to touch and tease her soft lips in tender, biting kisses that made her muscles go rigid with sensation. Her hand caught at his shirt, searching for something to hold on to while she spun out of reality altogether. Her nails bit into his chest.

He groaned under his breath. "You'd be a handful," he whispered. "And if you were a different sort of woman, I'd accept with open arms the invitation you're making me right now."

"What…invitation?"

His nose rubbed against hers. "This one."

He brought his mouth down over her parted lips with real intent, feeling them open and shiver convulsively as he deepened the pressure. She whimpered, and the sound shot through him like fire. He abruptly drew back.

His breathing was a little quick, but his expression showed none of the turmoil that kissing her had aroused in him.

She was slower to recover. Her face was flushed, and her mouth was red, swollen from the hard pressure of his lips. She looked at him with wide-eyed surprise.

"You're like a little violet under a doorstep," he commented quietly. "A lovely surprise waiting to be discovered."

She couldn't find the words to express what she felt.

He touched her soft mouth. "Don't worry about it. Someday the right man will come along. I'm not him."

"Why did you do that?" she whispered in a choked voice.

"Because you wanted me to, Jessica," he drawled. "You've watched me for months, wondering how it would feel if I kissed you. Okay. Now you know."

Her eyes darkened with something like pain. She averted them.

"What did you expect?" he mused, pulling the car back out into the road. "I'm not a teenager on his first date. I know exactly what to do with a woman. But you're off-limits, sweetheart. I don't make promises I can't keep."

"I haven't asked you to marry me, have I?" she asked, bouncing back.

He smiled appreciatively. "Not yet."

"And you can hold your breath until I do." She pushed back a disheveled strand of hair. "I'm not getting mixed up with you."

"You like kissing me."

She glared at him. "I like kissing my cat, too, McCallum," she said maliciously.

"Ouch!"

She nodded her head curtly. "Now how arrogant do you feel?"

He chuckled. "Well, as one of my history professors was fond of saying, I've always felt that arrogance was a very admirable quality in a man."

She rolled her eyes.

* * *

He drove back into town, but he didn't stop at her office. He kept going until he reached the Hip Hop Café, a small restaurant on the southeast corner of Amity Lane and Center.

She glanced at him uncertainly.

"If I haven't eaten, I know you haven't," he explained.

"All right. But I pay for my own food."

His eyes slowly wandered over her face. "I like independence," he said unexpectedly.

"Do I care?" she asked with mock surprise.

He smiled. "Fix your lipstick before we go inside, or everyone's going to know what we've been doing."

She wouldn't blush, she wouldn't blush, she wouldn't…!

All the same, her cheeks were pink in the compact mirror she used as she reapplied her lipstick and powdered her nose.

McCallum had taken the time to wipe the traces of pink off his own firm mouth with his handkerchief.

"Next time, I'll get rid of that lipstick before I start," he murmured.

"Oh, you'd be so lucky!" she hissed.

He lifted an eyebrow over wise, soft eyes. "Or you would. It gets better, the deeper you go. You cried out, and I hadn't even touched you. Imagine, Jessica, how it would feel if I did."

She was out of the car before he finished speaking.

She should go back to her office and leave him standing there. He was wicked to tease her about something she couldn't control. It didn't occur to her that he might be overcompensating for the desire he'd felt with her. Experienced he might be, but it had been a while since he'd had a woman and Jessica went right to his head. He hadn't realized it was going to be so fulfilling to kiss her. And it seemed to be addictive, because it was all he could think about.

"I won't let you torment me," she said, walking ahead of him to the door. "And before we go any farther, you'd better remember that Whitehorn isn't that big. Everybody knows everybody else's business. If I go in there with you, people are going to talk about us."

He had one hand in his pocket, the other on the door handle. He searched her eyes. "I know," he said quietly. He opened the door deliberately.

It was a quiet, companionable lunch. There were a few interested looks, including a sad one from a young waitress who had a hopeless crush on McCallum. But people were discreet enough not to stare at them.

"After all, we could be talking over a case," Jessica said.

He frowned at her. "Does it really matter?" he asked. "You're very sensitive to gossip. Why?"

She shrugged, averting her eyes. "Nobody likes being talked about."

"I don't know that I ever have been since I've come back," he said idly. He sipped his coffee. "And with your spotless reputation, it's hardly likely to think that you have," he added with a chuckle.

She picked up her coffee cup, steadying it with her other hand. "Thank you for helping me with Amy and Ben."

"Did I have a choice? I wonder if there isn't a law against deputy sheriffs being kidnapped by overconscientious social workers. And while we're on the subject of laws, that one about under-age marriages is one I'll have to look up or ask Hensley about. I've never had cause to use it before."

"You may again. We've had several cases like Amy and Ben over the years."

"What if she is pregnant?" he asked.

"Then she'll have choices and people to help her make them."

He glared at her.

"I know that look," she said softly. "I even understand it. But you have to consider that sometimes what's best for a young girl isn't necessarily what you feel is right."

"What if I lost my head one dark night and got you pregnant, Jessica?" He leaned back, his eyes narrowed. "What would you do in Amy's place?"

The color that rushed into her face was a revelation. She spilled a bit of coffee onto the table.

"Well, well," he murmured softly.

She put the cup down and mopped up the coffee with napkins. "You love shocking me, don't you?"

"Never mind the shock. Answer me. What would you do?"

She bit her lower lip. "The correct thing…"

He caught her hand and held it tight in his. "Not the correct thing, or the sensible thing, or even the decent thing. What would *you* do?" he asked evenly.

"Oh, I'd keep it," she said, angry at being pushed into answering a question that would not, could not, ever arise. It hurt her to remember how barren she was. "I'm just brimming over with motherly instincts, old-fashioned morality and an overworked sense of duty. But what I'm trying to make you see is that regardless of my opinion, I have no right to force my personal sense of right and wrong on the rest of the world!"

He forgot the social issue in the heat of the moment, as he allowed himself to wonder how it would feel to create a child with Jessica. It made him feel…odd.

Jessica saw the speculation in his eyes and all her old inadequacies came rushing back. "McCallum," she began, wondering whether or not to tell him about her condition.

His fingers linked with hers, his thumb smoothing over them. "You're twenty-five, aren't you? I'm ten years older."

"Yes, I know. McCallum…"

His eyes lifted to catch hers. "My first name is Sterling," he said.

"That's an unusual name. Was it in your family?"

He shrugged. "My mother never said." Memories of

his mother filled his mind. He withdrew, mentally and physically. He pulled his hand slowly away from Jessica's. "Maybe it was the name of her favorite brand of gin, who knows?"

She grimaced, hating that pain in his eyes. She wanted to soothe him, to comfort him.

He looked up and saw the expression on her face. It made him furious.

"I don't need pity," he said through gritted teeth.

"Is that how I looked? I'm sorry. It disturbs me to see how badly your past has affected you, that's all." She smiled. "I know. I'm a hopeless do-gooder. But think, McCallum—if you'd had someone who really cared what happened to you, wouldn't it have changed your whole life?"

He averted his eyes. "Facts are facts. We can't go back and change the past."

"I know that. If we could, think how many people would leap at the chance."

"True," he agreed.

She studied him over her cup. "This town must hold some bad memories for you. Why did you come back after all these years?"

"I got tired of my job," he replied. "I can't even talk about it, do you know? It was all classified. Let's just say that I got into a situation I couldn't handle for the first time in my life, and I got out. I don't regret it. I manage better here than I ever dreamed I would. I'm not rich, but I'm comfortable, and I like my job and the people I work with. Besides," he added, "the memories weren't all bad. I have a few good ones tucked away. They keep me going when I need them."

"And was there ever a special woman?" she asked, deliberately not looking at him.

He cocked an eyebrow. "*Women,* plural," he replied. "Not just one woman. They all knew the score. I made sure of it and I'm a loner. I don't want to change."

Jessica felt a vague disappointment.

"Were you hoping?" he taunted.

She glared at him. "For what? You, with a bow around your neck on Christmas morning? It's a long time until Christmas, McCallum, and you'd look silly in gift wrapping."

"Probably so." He studied her. "I wonder how you'd look in a long red stocking?"

"Dead, because that's the only way I'd ever end up in one. Heavens, look at the time! I've got my desk stacked halfway to the ceiling. I have to go!"

"So do I," he agreed. "The days are never long enough to cope with all the paperwork, even in my job."

"In everyone's job. God knows how many trees die every day to satisfy bureaucrats. Know what I think they do with all those triplicate copies? I think they make confetti and store it for parades."

"I wouldn't doubt it." He pushed away his empty

cup, stood up, laid a bill on the table, picked up the check and walked to the counter with it.

Jessica dug out a five-dollar bill and paid her share.

"Late lunch, huh, McCallum?" the waitress asked with an inviting smile.

"Yeah." He smiled back at her. "Thanks, Daisy."

She colored prettily. She was barely twenty, red-headed, cute and totally infatuated with McCallum.

He opened the door for Jessica and walked her back to his car.

"Thanks for your help," she told him with genuine appreciation. "Those kids needed more of a talking to than I could give them. There's something about a uniform…" she added with a gleam in her eyes. Of course she was kidding; McCallum, a plainclothesman, wasn't wearing a uniform.

"Tell me about it." He'd already discovered that uniforms attracted women. It was something most career law-enforcement officers learned how to deal with early.

"Have you found out anything about Jennifer?" she asked on the way back to her office.

He detailed the bits and pieces he'd been following up. "But with no luck. Do you know any midwives around the community?" he asked. "Someone who would be able to deliver a child and could do it without telling half the world?"

Jessica pursed her lips. "One or two women come to mind. I'll look into it."

"Thanks."

He stopped at her office and waited, with the car idling, for her to get out.

"I'll let you know how things go with Amy," she offered.

He looked at her with an expression that bordered on dislike. It had flattered him that she kept asking for his help, and she seemed to like his company. But he liked kissing her too much, and that made him irritable. He didn't want a social worker to move into his life. He was weakening toward her, and he couldn't afford that. "I don't remember asking for a follow-up report," he said, deliberately being difficult.

It didn't faze Jessica, who was used to him. His bad humor bounced off her. That kiss hadn't, of course, but she had to remember that he was a loner and keep things in perspective. She could mark that lapse down to experience. She knew she wouldn't forget it anytime soon, but she had to keep her eyes off McCallum.

"You're so cynical, McCallum," she said heavily. "Haven't you ever heard that old saying about no man being an island?"

"I read John Donne in college," he replied. "I can be an island if I please."

She pursed her lips again, surveying him with marked interest. "If you really were an island, you'd have barbed wire strung around the trees and land mines on the beaches."

She went inside, aware of the deep masculine laughter she left behind her.

The abandoned baby, Jennifer, had been placed in care, and Jessica couldn't help going to see her. She was living temporarily as a ward of the court with a local family that seemed to thrive on anyone's needful children.

"We can't have any of our own, you see," Mabel Darren said with a grin. She was in her mid-thirties, dark and bubbly, and it didn't take a clairvoyant to know that she loved children. She had six of them, all from broken homes or orphaned, ranging in age from a toddler to a teen.

The house was littered, but clean. The social-services office had to check it out periodically to comply with various regulations, but there had never been any question of the Darrens' ability to provide for their charges. And if ever children were loved, these underprivileged ones were.

"Isn't she a little angel?" Mabel asked when Jessica had the sweet-smelling infant in her arms.

"Oh, yes," Jessica said, feeling a terrible pain as she cuddled the child. She would never know the joy of childbirth, much less that of watching a baby grow to adulthood. She would be alone all her life.

Mabel would have understood, but Jessica could never bring herself to discuss her anguish with anyone. She carried Jennifer to the rocking chair and sat down with her, oblivious to the many other duties that were supposed to be demanding her attention.

The older woman just smiled. "It's time for her bottle. Would you like to feed her while you're here? Then I could get on with my dirty dishes," she added. She knew already that if she could make Jessica think she was helping, the social worker was much more likely to do what she really wanted to.

"If it would help," Jessica said. Her soft, dark eyes were on the baby's face and she touched the tiny head, the hands, the face with fingers that trembled. She'd never known such a profound hunger in her life, and tears stung her eyes.

As if the baby sensed her pain, her big eyes opened and she stared up at Jessica, unblinking. She made a soft gurgling noise in her throat. With a muffled cry, Jessica cuddled Jennifer close and started the chair rocking. At that moment, she would have given anything—anything!—for this tiny precious thing to be her very own.

Mabel's footsteps signaled her approach. Jessica composed herself just before the other woman reappeared with a bottle. She managed to feed the baby and carry on a pleasant conversation with Mabel, apparently unruffled by the experience. But deep inside, she was devastated. Something about Jennifer accentuated all the terrible feelings of inadequacy and made her child hungry. She'd never wanted anything as much as she wanted the abandoned infant.

After she fed the baby, she went back to the office, where she was broody and quiet for the rest of the day.

She was so silent that Bess, who worked in the outer office, stuck her auburn head in the door to inquire if her boss was sick.

"No, I'm all right, but thanks," Jessica said dully. "It's been a long day, that's all."

"Well, you got to have lunch with Sterling McCallum," Bess mused. "I wouldn't call that tedious. I dress up, I wear sexy perfume, but he never gives me a second look. Is he really that formidable and business-like *all* the time?" she asked with a keen stare.

Jessica's well-schooled features gave nothing away. She smiled serenely. "If I ever find out, you'll be the first to know. It was a business lunch, Bess, not a date," she added.

"Oh, you stick-in-the-mud," she muttered. "A gorgeous man like that, and all you want to talk about is work! I'd have him on his back in the front seat so fast…!"

Shocking images presented themselves, but with Jessica, not Bess, imprisoning Sterling McCallum on the seat of his car. She had to stop thinking of him in those terms! "Really, Bess!" she muttered.

"Jessica, you do know what century this is?" Bess asked gently. "You know, the nineties, uninhibited sex?"

"AIDS?" Jessica added.

Bess made a soft sound. "Well, I didn't mean that you don't have to be careful. But McCallum strikes me as the sort of man who would be. I'll bet he's always properly equipped."

Jessica's face had gone scarlet and she stood up abruptly.

"I'm just leaving for home!" Bess said quickly, all too aware that she'd overstepped the mark. "See you tomorrow!"

She closed the door and ran for it. Jessica was even-tempered most of the time, but she, too, could be formidable when she lost her cool.

Jessica restrained a laugh at the speed with which Bess took to her heels. It was just as well not to let employees get too complacent, she decided, as she opened another file and went back to work.

It was after dark and pouring rain when she decided to go home. Meriwether would be wanting his supper, and she was hungry enough herself. The work would still be here, waiting, in the morning. But it had taken her mind off Baby Jennifer, which was a good thing.

She locked up the office and got into her yellow pickup as quickly as possible. Her umbrella, as usual, was at home. She had one in the office, too, but she'd forgotten it. She was wet enough without trying to go back and get it. She fumbled the key into the ignition, locked her door and started the vehicle.

The engine made the most ghastly squealing noise. It didn't help to remember McCallum's grim warning about trouble ahead if she didn't get it seen to.

But the mechanic's shop was closed, and so were all

the service stations. The convenience store was open, and it had self-service gas pumps, but nobody who worked inside would know how to replace a fan belt. In fact, Tammie Jane was working the counter tonight, and the most complicated thing she knew how to do was change her nail polish.

With a long sigh, Jessica pulled the truck out onto the highway and said a silent prayer that she would be able to make it home before the belt broke. The squeal that usually vanished when she went faster only got worse tonight.

The windshield wipers were inadequate, too. A big leaf had gotten caught in the one on the driver's side, smearing the water rather than removing it. Jessica groaned out loud at her bad luck. It had been a horrible day altogether, and not just because of the predicament she was in now.

She pulled onto the dirt road that led to her home. The rain was coming down harder. She had no idea how long it had been pouring, because she'd been so engrossed in her work. Now she saw the creek ahead and wondered if she'd even be able to get across it. The water was very high. This was an old and worrying problem.

She gunned the engine and shot across, barely missing another struggling motorist, her elderly CB-radio-fanatic neighbor. He waved to her as he went past, but she was too occupied with trying to see ahead to really look at him. She almost made it up the hill, but at that very moment, the fan belt decided to give up the ghost. It snapped and the engine raced, but nothing happened. The truck slid back to the bottom of the hill beside the wide, rising creek, and the engine went dead.

Six

Jessica sat in the truck without moving, muttering under her breath. She hoped that her eccentric neighbor had noticed her plight and alerted someone in town on his CB radio, but whether or not he'd seen her slide back down the hill was anyone's guess.

She decided after a few minutes that she was going to be stranded unless she did something. The creek was rising steadily. She was terrified of floods. If she didn't get up that hill, god only knew what might happen to her when the water rose higher. The rain showed no sign of slackening.

She opened the door and got out, becoming soaked within the first couple of minutes. She made a rough sound in her throat and let out an equally rough word

to go with it. Stupid old truck! She should have listened
to McCallum.

She managed to get the hood up, but it did no good.
There was no source of light except the few patches of
sky on the horizon that weren't black as thunder. She
didn't even have a flashlight. Well, she had one—but the
battery was dead. She'd meant to replace it....

The deep drone of an engine caught her attention.
She turned, blinded by headlights, hoping against hope
that it was her elderly neighbor. He could give her a ride
home, at least.

A huge red-and-black Bronco with antennas all over it
and a bar of lights on top swept up beside her and stopped.
She recognized it from McCallum's house. It had been
sitting in the garage next to the patrol car he used when he
was on call at night. He got out of it, wearing a yellow rain
slicker. The rain seemed to slacken as he approached her.

"Nice wheels," she commented.

"I like it," he replied. "Fan belt broke, huh?"

She glowered, shivering in the rain. "Terrific guess."

"No help here, until I can get a new belt and put it
on for you. Nothing's open this late." He closed the
hood and marched her around to the passenger side of
the Bronco. "Climb in."

He helped her into the big vehicle and she sat, shivering, on the vinyl seat while, with the four-wheel drive
in operation, he drove effortlessly up the muddy hill and
on to her cabin.

"What were you doing out at this time of night anyway?" he asked.

"Trying to get stranded in the rain," she told him.

He glared at her.

"I was working late." She sneezed.

"Get in there and take a bath."

"I had planned to. Have you...had supper?" she added, without looking at him.

"Not yet."

She touched the door handle. "I have a pot of soup in the refrigerator. I could make some cornbread to go with it."

"If you could make some coffee, I'd be delighted to join you. I'd just got off duty when I monitored a call about a stranded motorist."

She grinned, because she knew which motorist he meant. "Done." She got out and left him to follow.

The minute he walked in the door, Meriwether, having come to meet his mistress, bristled and began spitting viciously at the newcomer.

"I like you, too, pal," McCallum muttered as he and the cat had a glaring contest.

"Meri, behave yourself!" Jessica fussed.

"If you'll show me what the soup's in, I'll start heating it while you're in the shower," he offered.

She led him into the kitchen, dripping everywhere, and got out the big pot of soup while he hung up his drenched slicker.

"I'll make the cornbread when I get back. You could preheat the oven," she added, and told him what temperature to set it.

"Okay. Where's the coffee?"

She showed him the filters and coffee and how to work the pot. Then she rushed down the hall to the bathroom.

Ten minutes later, clean and presentable in a sweat-shirt and jeans, with her hair hanging in damp strands down her back, she joined him in the kitchen.

"You'll catch a cold," he murmured, glancing at her from his seat at the table with a steaming cup of black coffee. "Sit down for a minute and I'll pour you a cup."

"I'll make the cornbread first," she said. "It won't take a minute."

And it didn't She put it in the preheated oven to bake and then sat down across from McCallum to sip her coffee. He was wearing a brown plaid shirt, with jeans and boots. He always looked clean and neat, even when he was drenched, she thought, and wondered if his military training had a lot to do with it.

"Do you always keep your house this hot?" he asked, unfastening the top buttons of his shirt.

"I don't have air-conditioning," she explained apologetically. "But I can turn on the fan."

"Are you cool?"

She shook her head. "I'm rather cold-blooded, I'm afraid. But if you're too hot…"

"Leave it. It's probably the coffee." He leaned back.

The action pulled his shirt away from his chest and she got a glimpse of the thick mat of curling black hair that covered it.

She averted her eyes in the direction of the stove and watched it fanatically, not daring to look at him again. He was devastating like that, so attractive physically that he made her toes curl.

He saw the look he was getting. It made his heart race. She was certainly less sophisticated than most women he knew, but she still made him hungry in a new and odd sort of way.

"You said you monitored a stranded motorist's call?" she asked curiously.

"Yes. Your neighbor called the office on his mobile unit, and when I heard where the stranded motorist was, I told Dispatch that I'd respond." He grinned at her. "I knew who it was and what was wrong before I got here."

She took an audible breath. "Well, it might have been something besides the fan belt," she said.

"You're stubborn."

"I meant to have it checked," she defended herself. "I got busy."

"Next time you'll know better, won't you?"

"I hate it when you use that tone," she muttered. "I'm not brain dead just because I'm a woman!"

His eyebrows raised. "Did I imply that you were?"

"You have an attitude...."

"So do you," he shot back. "Defensive and standoffish. I'd have told a man no differently than I told you that your fan belt needed replacing. The difference is that a man would have listened."

She put her coffee cup down hard and opened her mouth to speak just as the beeper on the oven's timer went off.

He got up with her and took the soup off the burner while she checked the cornbread in the oven. It was nicely browned, just right.

She was silent while she dished up the abbreviated meal, and while they ate it.

"You're a good cook, Jessie," he commented when he'd finished his second helping. "Who taught you?"

"My grandmother," she said. "My mother was not a good cook. She tried, God bless her, but we never gained weight around here." She pushed back her bowl. "You're handy enough in a kitchen yourself."

"Had to be," he said simply. "My mother was never sober enough to cook. If I hadn't learned, we'd both have starved. Not that she ate much. She drank most of her meals."

"You sound so bitter," she said gently.

"I *am* bitter," he shot back. He crossed his long legs, brushing at a smudge of mud on one polished black boot. "She robbed me of my childhood." His eyes sought her. "Isn't that what most victims of child abuse tell you— that what they mourn most is the loss of childhood?"

She nodded. "That's the worst of it. The pain and bitterness go on for a long time, even after therapy. You can't remake the past, McCallum. The scars don't go away, even if the patient can be made to restructure the way he or she thinks about the experience."

He turned his coffee cup around, his eyes on the white china soup bowl, now empty. "I never did what young boys usually get to do—play sports, join the Boy Scouts, go on trips, go to parties... From the time I was old enough, I did nothing except look after my mother, night after drunken night." His lean hand contacted absently on the bowl. "I used to hope she'd die."

"That's very normal," she assured him.

His broad shoulders rose and fell. "She did die, though in jail. I had her arrested when it all got too much after she attacked me one night. She was convicted of child abuse, sent to jail, and she died there when I was in my early teens. I was put to work as a hired hand for any family that would take me in. I had a room in a bunkhouse or in the barn, never with the family. I spent most of my life as an outsider looking in, until I was old enough to join the service. The uniform gave me a little self-esteem. As I grew older, I learned that my situation wasn't all that rare."

"Sadly, it isn't," she told him. "Sterling, what about your father?"

Her use of his first name made him feel warm inside. He smiled at her. "What about him?"

"Did he die?"

"Beats me," he said quietly. "I never found out who he was. I'm not sure she knew."

The implications of that statement were devastating. She winced.

"Feeling sorry for me all over again?" he murmured gently. "I don't need pity, Jessie. I've come to grips with it over the years. Plenty of people had it worse."

She traced the rim of her coffee cup soberly. "I'm sorry that it was that way for you."

"Different from your childhood, I imagine."

"Oh, yes. I was loved and wanted, and petted. I don't suppose I had a single bad experience in my whole childhood."

"They say we carry our childhood around with us, like luggage. I'll have to worry about not being too rough on my kids. You'll be just the opposite."

She felt sick inside, and tried not to show it. "Have you managed to find out anything else about little Jenny?" she asked, changing the subject.

"Nothing except dead ends," he had to admit. "I did find one new lead, but it didn't work out. How about you? Anything on the midwives?"

"I've spoken to two, but they say they don't know anything." She twirled her spoon on the tablecloth. "I'm not sure they'd tell me if they did," she added, looking up. "Sometimes they get in trouble for helping with deliveries, especially if something goes wrong. What if the mother died giving birth, Sterling?"

"That's a thought." His lips pursed. "I might check into any recent deaths involving childbirth."

"It might not lead to anything at all, but someone has to know about her. I mean, she didn't come from under a cabbage leaf."

He chuckled. "I don't think so."

She liked the sound of his laughter. She smiled as she got up to put the dishes in the sink.

"No dishwasher?" he teased as he helped.

"Of course I have a dishwasher—myself." She smiled at him. "I'll put these in to soak and do them later."

"Do them now, while I'm here to help you."

She did, because it would keep him here that much longer. She enjoyed his company far too much. She filled the sink with soapy water, while outside the rain continued steadily, broken occasionally by a rumble of thunder. "Were you always so bossy?" she asked as she washed a plate and handed it to him to be rinsed.

"I suppose so," he confessed. "That's force of habit. I was the highest-ranking officer in my group."

"What did you do in Naval Intelligence?"

He put the plate in the dish drainer and leaned toward her. "That's classified," he whispered.

"Well, excuse me for asking!" she teased.

His dark eyes searched hers. "I like the way you look when you smile," he commented absently. "It lights up your whole face."

"You hardly ever smile."

"I do when I'm with you. Haven't you noticed?"

She laughed self-consciously. "Yes, but I thought it was because you find me tedious." She washed another few dishes and passed them to him.

He rinsed them and then began drying, because there were none left to be washed. "I find you disturbing," he corrected quietly.

She let the water out of the sink and took a second cloth, helping to dry the few dishes. "Because I'm forever dragging you into awkward situations?"

"Not quite."

They finished drying the dishes and Jessica put them away. She hung up the kitchen towels. Lightning flashed outside the window, followed by a renewal of pelting rain and a deep, vibrating rumble of thunder.

"Are you afraid of thunderstorms?" he asked her.

"A little."

He moved closer, his face filling her whole line of vision. "Are you afraid of me?" he continued.

Her eyes slid over his face, lingering on his firm mouth and chin. "That would depend on what you wanted from me," she countered bluntly.

"That's forthright enough," he said. "All right, cards on the table. Suppose I want you sexually?"

She didn't drop her eyes. "I don't want sex."

His gaze narrowed. "Because of what happened to you?" he guessed.

"Not entirely." She stared at the opening in his shirt,

feeling her heartbeat increase as the clean cologne-and-soap scent of his body drifted into her nostrils. "It's mainly a matter of morality, I guess. And I'm not equipped for casual affairs, either. This is a small town. I...don't like gossip. I've always tried to live in such a way that people wouldn't think less of me."

"I see," he said slowly.

She shifted her shoulders. "No, you don't. You've been away so long maybe you've forgotten what it's really like." Her eyes were faintly pleading. "I like my life the way it is. I don't want to complicate it. I'm sorry."

His lean hands caught her waist gently and brought her against the length of his body. He stopped her instinctive withdrawal.

"Hush," she whispered. "Be still."

"What are...you doing?"

"I'm showing you that it's too late," he replied. His big hands smoothed her back up to her shoulder blades. "You want me. I want you. We can slow it down, but we can't stop it. Deep inside, you don't want to stop me." His gaze dropped to her soft mouth, and he watched her lips part. "You've been handled brutally. But you've never been touched with tenderness. I'm going to show you how it feels."

"I'm not sure that I want to know," she whispered.

He bent toward her. "Let's see."

Her fingers went up to touch his lips, staying their

downward movement. Her eyes were wide and soft and faintly pleading. "Don't…hurt me," she said.

He moved her hand to his shirtfront and scowled. "Do you think I want to?"

"No, I don't mean physically. I mean…" She searched for words. "Sterling, I can't play games. I'm much too intense. It would be better if we were just friends."

He tilted her chin up and held her eyes. "Think about what you're saying," he said gently. "I know about your past. I know that you've been assaulted, that you don't date anyone. I even know that you're half-afraid of me. Considering all that, do you think I'm the sort of man who would tease you?"

She looked perplexed. Her hand had moved somehow into the opening where the buttons were unfastened. She felt the curly tangle of thick chest hair over warm, hard muscle. It was difficult to concentrate when all she wanted to do was touch him, test his maleness.

"Well, no," she confessed.

"I don't play games with women," he said flatly. "I'm straightforward. Sometimes too much so. I want you, but I'd never force you or put you in a position where you couldn't say no." He laughed mirthlessly. "Or don't you realize that I've been in that position myself?"

Her brows jerked together as she tried to puzzle out what he was saying.

"When one of my foster mothers got drunk enough,"

he said slowly, bitterly, "anything male would do. She tried to seduce me one night."

Her heart ached for him. What a distasteful, sickening experience it would have been for a young boy. "Oh, Sterling!" she said sadly.

The distaste dominated his expression. "I knocked her out of the bed and left the house. The next morning, we had it out. I told her exactly what would happen if she ever tried it again. I was almost as big then as I am now, you see. She couldn't force me." His hands let her go and he moved away.

She'd come across the same situation so many times, with so many families. It was amazing how many children suffered such traumas and never told, because of the shock and shame.

She moved closer to him, but she didn't touch him. She knew very well that abused children had real problems about being touched by other people sometimes—especially when something reminded them of the episodes—unless it was through their own choice. The scars were long lasting.

"You never told anyone," she guessed.

He wouldn't look at her. "No."

"Not even your caseworker?"

He shrugged. "He was the sort who wouldn't have believed me. And I had too much pride to beg for credibility."

She mourned the help he could have gotten from someone with a little more compassion.

"I've never told anyone," he continued, glancing down at her. "Amazing that I could tell you."

"Not really," she said, smiling. "I think you could tell me anything."

His face tautened. It was true. He would never balk at divulging his darkest secrets to this woman, because she had an open, loving heart. She wouldn't ridicule or judge, and she wouldn't repeat anything he said.

"I think I must have that sort of face," she continued, tongue-in-cheek, "because total strangers come up and talk to me about the most shocking things. I actually had a man ask me what to do about impotence."

He chuckled, his bad memories temporarily driven away. "And what did you tell him?"

"That a doctor would be a more sensible choice for asking advice," she returned. Her eyes searched his dark, hard face. "Sex was really hard for you the first time, wasn't it?" she asked bluntly.

Again his face tautened. "Yes."

She glanced away, folding her arms over her breasts. "I wasn't a child when I had my bad experience, but it made the thought of intimacy frightening to me. I'm realistic enough to know that it would be different with someone I cared about, but all I can see is the way he was. He reminded me of an animal."

"Do I?"

She turned quickly. "Don't be absurd!"

One eyebrow quirked. "Well, that's something."

She went back to him, looking up solemnly into his face. "I find *you* very disturbing," she confessed. "Physically, I mean. I guess that's why I shy away from you sometimes."

He traced her smooth cheek with a steely forefinger. "I don't think I've ever known anyone as honest as you."

"I hate lies. Don't you?"

"I hear enough of them. Nobody I've ever arrested has been guilty. It was a frame-up, or they didn't mean to, or somebody talked them into it."

"I know what you mean."

The exploring finger reached her mouth and traced its soft bow shape gently. His jaw tightened. She could hear the heavy breath that passed through his nostrils as his eyes began to darken and narrow.

"Why don't you unfasten my shirt and put your hands on me?" he asked huskily.

Her face colored vividly. "I don't know if that would be a good idea."

"It's the best one I've had tonight," he assured her. "No games. Honest. I want to make love to you a little, that's all. I won't let it get too far."

She put her hands against his shirtfront, torn between what she wanted to do and what was sensible.

"It's hard for me, with women," he said roughly. "Does that reassure you any?"

She smiled gently. "Will it make you angry if I confess that it does?"

He bent and his smiling mouth brushed against hers. "Probably. Open your mouth."

She obeyed him like a sleepwalker, but he soon brought every single nerve she had singing to life. Her hands slid under the shirt and over the thick tangle of hair that covered him, past male nipples that hardened at her touch. He moaned softly and pulled her closer. She sighed into his mouth as he deepened the kiss and made her knees go weak with the passion he kindled in her slender body.

"It isn't enough," he said in a strained tone. He bent and lifted her, his gaze reassuring as she opened startled eyes. "I want to lie down with you," he whispered as he carried her to the sofa. "I have to get closer, Jessie. Closer than this."

"It's dangerous," she managed through swollen lips.

"Life is dangerous." He put her down on the sofa, full length, and stretched out alongside her. "I won't hurt you. I swear to God, I won't. All it will take is one word, when you want me to stop."

His mouth traced hers. "And what…if I can't say it?" she whispered brokenly.

"I'll say it for you…."

He kissed her until she trembled, but even then he didn't touch her intimately or attempt to carry their lovemaking to greater depths. He lifted his head and looked down at her with tenderness and bridled passion. With her long hair loose around her face and her lips swollen from his kisses, her dark eyes wide and soft and dazed, he thought he'd never seen anything so beautiful in all his life.

"Are you stopping?" she whispered unsteadily.

"I think I should," he mused, managing to project a self-assurance he didn't really feel. His lower body ached.

"But we haven't done anything except kiss each other…." She stopped abruptly when she realized what she was saying.

He chuckled wickedly. "Jessie, if I push up that sweatshirt, we're both going to be in trouble. Because, frankly, it shows that you aren't wearing anything under it."

She followed his interested gaze and saw two hard peaks outlined vividly against the soft material. Scarlet faced, she got to her feet. "Well!"

He sat back on the sofa, watching her with smug, delighted eyes. She aroused an odd protectiveness in him that he'd never felt with another woman. She was unique in his shattered life. He wanted her, but it went far beyond desire.

"Don't be embarrassed," he said gently. "I didn't say it with any cruel intent. It delights me that you can want me, Jessie." He hesitated. "It delights me that I can want you. I wasn't sure…"

She searched his hard face. "Yes?" she prompted gently.

He got up and went to her slowly, secrets in his eyes. She pushed back the glorious cloud of her hair and then reached up to touch his sculptured cheek. "Tell me," she coaxed.

He brought her hand to his lips. "I exaggerated when I told you there had been a parade of women through my bed," he said quietly.

Her eyes were solemn, steady, questioning.

His shoulders moved restlessly. He looked tormented. He tried to tell her, but the words wouldn't come.

Her fingers traced his hard mouth. "It's all right." She pulled his head down and kissed his eyes closed. He shivered. "My dear," she whispered. Her mouth traced his and softly kissed his lips, feeling them open and press down, responding with a sudden feverish need. He pulled her close and increased the pressure, groaning as she gave in to him without a single protest.

He let her go slowly, his tall, fit body taut with desire and need as he looked down at her hungrily.

"I've never been with anyone like you," he said flatly. "Because of the way I grew up, I always equated sex with a certain kind of woman," he said huskily. "So that's where I went, when I had to have it." He sighed heavily. "Not that I was ever careless, Jessie."

She bit her lip, trying not to remember Bess's taunt.

"What is it?" he asked suspiciously.

"I can't tell you. You'll get conceited."

His eyebrows arched. He cocked his head. "Come on."

"A girl I know made the comment that she thought you'd be absolute heaven to make love with, and that she'd bet you were always prepared."

He chuckled softly. "Did she? Who?"

"I'll never tell!"

He pursed his lips, amused. "As it happens, she was right." He bent and brushed her mouth with his. "On both counts," he whispered and nipped her lower lip.

She smiled under his lips. "I know. About the first count, anyway."

"You can take my word for the other. How about supper tomorrow night?"

She stared at him blankly. "What?"

"I want to take you out on a date," he explained. "One of those things where a man and woman spend time together, and at the end of the evening, do what we've already done."

"Oh."

His eyebrow lifted as he fastened his shirt. "Well?"

Her face lit up. "I'd love to!"

He smiled. "So would I. Thanks for supper." He moved to the door and glanced back. She was ruffled and flustered. He liked knowing that he'd made her that way. "I'll send the mechanic over first thing in the morning to see about that fan belt. And I'll come and drive you to work."

"You don't have to," she declared breathlessly.

"I want to." The way he said it projected other images, exciting ones. She laughed inanely, captivated by the look on his dark face.

"I'd better go," he murmured dryly. "Good night, Jessie."

"Good night."

He closed the door gently behind him. "Lock it!" he added from outside.

She rushed forward and threw the lock into place. A minute later she heard deep laughter and the sound of his booted feet going down the steps.

Seven

The restaurant was crowded, and heads turned from all directions when Jessica, in a neat-fitting burgundy dress with her hair loose around her shoulders, walked in with McCallum, who was wearing slacks and a sports coat.

"I told you people would notice that we're together," she said under her breath as they were seated.

"I didn't mind the last time, and I don't mind now," he murmured, smiling. "Do you?"

She smiled back. "Not at all."

The waitress brought menus, poured water into glasses and went away to give them time to decide what to order.

"Why…Miss Larson!"

Jessica looked up. Bess, one of her caseworkers, and

a good-looking young man who worked in the bank had paused by their table.

"Hello, Bess," Jessica said, smiling. "How are you?"

"Fine! Don't you look nice? Hi, McCallum," she added, letting her blue eyes sweep over him in pure flirtation. "You look nice, too!"

"Thanks."

"Bess, the waitress is gesturing to us," the young man prompted. He was giving McCallum a nervous look. Probably it was the fact that McCallum was in law enforcement that disturbed him. Lawmen were set apart from the rest of the world, Jessica had discovered over the years. But it could have been the way Bess was looking at the older man. Jessica had to admit that McCallum was sensuous and handsome enough to fit any woman's dream. Compared to him, Bess's date seemed very young, and he was undoubtedly jealous.

"Oh, sure, Steve. Good to see you both!" she said breezily, leading him away.

"She thinks you're a hunk," Jessica said without thinking, then bit her lip.

His eyebrows lifted. "So?" Now he knew who'd made the comment she'd related at her cabin.

"She's very young, of course," she added mischievously.

"No, she isn't," he countered. "In fact, she's only a year younger than you. Nice figure, too."

Jessica fought down an unfamiliar twinge of jealousy. She fumbled with her silverware. Nobody disturbed her like McCallum did.

He reached across the table and caught her hand in his, sending thrills of pleasure up her arm that made her heart race. "I didn't mean it like that. Jessie, if I were interested in your co-worker, why would I spend half my free time thinking about you?"

She smiled at him, thrown off balance by the look in his dark eyes. "Do you?" she asked. Her hand slipped and almost overturned her water glass. He righted it quickly, smiling patiently at her clumsiness. It wasn't like her to do such things.

"Hold tight, and I'll protect you from overturning things," he said, clasping her cold fingers in his. "We'll muddle through together. In my own way, I've got as many hang-ups and inhibitions as you have. But if we try, we can sort it out."

"Sort what out?" she echoed curiously.

He frowned. "Do you think I make a habit of taking women out? I'm thirty-five years old, and since I've been back here, I've lived like a hermit. I'm hungry for a woman…."

This time the glass went over. He called the waitress, who managed to clear away the water with no effort at all. She smiled indulgently at an embarrassed Jessica, who was abjectly apologetic.

She took their order and left. Across the restaurant,

Bess was giggling. Jessica looked at Sterling McCallum and knew in that moment that she loved him. She also knew that she could never marry him. He might not realize it now, but he'd want children one day. He was the sort of man who needed children to love and take care of. He'd make a good husband. Of course, marriage was obviously the last thing on his mind at the moment.

"Good God, woman," he muttered, shaking his head with indulgent amusement. "Will you just let me finish a sentence before you react like that? I don't have plans to ravish you. Okay? Now, move that glass aside before we have another mishap."

"I'm sorry. I'm just all thumbs."

"And I keep putting my foot in my mouth," he said ruefully. "What I was going to say, before the great water glass flood," he added with a grin at her flush, "was that it's time I started going out more. I like you. We'll keep it low-key."

She looked at the big, lean hand holding hers so gently. Her fingers moved over the back of it, tracing, savoring its strength and masculinity. "I like your hands," she said absently. "They're very sensitive, for such masculine ones." She thought about how they might feel on bare, soft skin and her lips parted as she exhaled with unexpected force.

His thumb eased into the damp palm of her hand and began to caress it, making her heart race all over again. "Yours are beautiful," he said, and the memory of how

her hands felt on his chest was still in his gaze when
he looked up.

She was holding her breath. She looked into his eyes,
and neither of them smiled. It was like lightning
striking. She could see what he was thinking. It was all
there in his dark gaze—the need and the hunger and the
ardent passion he felt for her.

"Uh, excuse me?"

They both looked up blankly as the waitress, smiling
wryly, waited for them to move their hands so she could
put the plates down.

"Sorry," Sterling mumbled.

The waitress didn't say a word, but her expression
spoke volumes.

"I think we're becoming obvious," he remarked to
Jessica as he picked up his fork, trying not to look
around at the interested glances they were getting from
Bess and Steve.

"Yes." She sounded pained, and looked even more
uncomfortable.

"Jessie?"

"Hmm?" She looked up.

He leaned forward. "I'm dying of frustrated passion
here. Eat fast, could you?"

She burst out laughing. It broke the tension and got
them through the rest of the meal.

But once he paid the check and they went out to the
parking lot and got into the Bronco, he didn't take her

straight home. He drove a little way past the cabin and pulled down a long, dark trail into the woods.

He locked his door, unfastened his seatbelt and then reached across her wordlessly to lock her own door and release her seatbelt as well.

His eyes in the darkness held a faint glitter. She could feel the quick, harsh rush of his breath on her forehead. She didn't protest. Her arms reached around his neck as he pulled her across his lap. When his mouth lowered, hers was ready, waiting.

They melted together, so hungry for each other that nothing else seemed to matter.

She'd never experienced kisses that weren't complete in themselves. He made her want more, much more. Every soft stroke of his hands against her back was arousing, even through the layers of fabric. The brush of his lips on hers didn't satisfy, it taunted and teased. He nibbled at the outside curves of her mouth with brief little touches that made her heart run wild. She clung to him, hoping that he might deepen the kiss on his own account, but he seemed to be waiting.

She reached up, finally, driven to the outskirts of desperation by the teasing that went on and on until she was taut as drawn rope with unsatisfied needs.

"Please!" she whispered brokenly, trying to pull his head down.

"It isn't enough, is it?" he asked calmly. "I hoped it might not be. Open your mouth, Jessica," he whispered against her lips as he shifted her even closer to his broad, warm chest. "And I'll show you just how hungry a kiss can make you feel."

It was devastating. She felt her breath become suspended, like her mind, as his lips fitted themselves to hers and began to move in slow, teasing touches that quickly grew harder and rougher and deeper. By the time his tongue probed at her lips, they opened eagerly for him. When his tongue went deep into her mouth, she arched up against him and groaned out loud.

Her response kindled a growing hunger in him. It had been a long time for him, and the helpless twisting motions of her breasts against him made him want to rip open her dress and take them in his hands and his mouth.

Without thinking of consequences, he made her open her mouth even farther under the crush of his, and his lean hand dropped to her bodice, teasing her breasts through the cloth until he felt the nipples become hard. Only then did he smooth the firm warmth of one and begin to caress it with his fingertips. When he caught the nipple deliberately in his thumb and forefinger, she cried out. He lifted his head to see why. As he'd suspected, it wasn't out of fear or pain.

She lay there, just watching him as he caressed her. He increased the gentle pressure of his fingers and she gasped as she looked into his eyes. A slow flush spread over her high cheekbones in the dimly lit interior.

He didn't say a word. He simply sat there, holding her

and looking down into her shadowed eyes. It was hard to breathe. Her body was soft in his arms and that pretty burgundy dress had buttons down the front. His eyes went past the hand that now lay possessively on her breast and he calculated how easy it would be to open the buttons and bare her breasts to his hungry mouth. But she was trembling, and his body was getting quickly out of control. Besides that, it was too soon for that sort of intimacy. He had to give her time to get used to the idea before he tried to further their relationship. It was important not to frighten her so that she backed away from him.

He moved his hand up and pushed back her disheveled hair with a soft smile. "Sorry," he murmured dryly. "I guess I let it go a little too far."

"It was my fault, too. You're...you're very potent," she said after a minute, feeling the swelling of her mouth from his hard kisses and the tingling of her breast where his hand had toyed with it. She still couldn't imagine that she'd really let him do that. But, oddly, she didn't feel embarrassed about it. It seemed somehow proper for McCallum to touch her like that, as if she belonged to him already.

He grinned at her expression. "You're potent yourself. And that being the case, I think I'd better get you home."

She fingered his collar. "Okay." Her hands traced down to his tie and the top button of his shirt.

"No," he said gently, staying her fingers. "I like having you touch me there too much," he murmured dryly. "Let's not tempt fate twice in one night."

She was a little disappointed, even though she knew he was right. It *was* too soon. But her eyes mirrored more than one emotion.

He watched those expressions chase across her face, his eyes tender, full of secrets. "How did you get under my skin?" he wondered absently.

She glowed with pleasure. "Have I?"

"Right down to the bone, when I wasn't looking. I don't know if I like it." He studied her for a long moment. "Trust comes hard to me. Don't ever lie to me, Jessica," he said unexpectedly. "I can forgive anything except that. I've been sold out once too often in the past. The scars go deep and they came from painful lessons. I can't bear lies."

She thought about being barren, and wondered if this would be the right time to tell him. But it wasn't a lie, was it? It was a secret, one she would get around to, if it ever became necessary to tell him. But right now they were just dating, just friends. She was overreacting. She smiled. "Okay. I promise that I'll never deliberately lie to you." That got her around the difficult hurdle of her condition. She wasn't lying. She just wasn't confessing. It was middle ground, and not really dishonest. Of course it wasn't.

He let go of her hand and started the vehicle, turning on the lights. He glanced sideways at her as he pulled the Bronco out into the road and drove back to her cabin. She might be afraid, but there was desire in her

as well. She wanted him. He had to keep that in mind
and not give up hope.

He stopped at her front steps. "I want to take you out
from time to time," he said firmly. "We can go out to
eat—as my budget allows," he added with a grin, "and
to movies. And I'd like to take you fishing and deer
tracking with me this fall."

"Oh, I'd enjoy that." She looked surprised and delighted. The radiance of her face made her so stunning
that he lost his train of thought for a minute.

He frowned. "Just don't go shopping for wedding
bands and putting announcements in the local paper,"
he said firmly. He held up a hand when she started,
flustered, to protest. "There's no use arguing about it,
my mind's made up. I do know that you make wonderful homemade bread, and that's a point in your favor,
but you mustn't rush me."

Her eyes brightened with wicked pleasure. "Oh, I
wouldn't dream of it," she said, entering into the spirit
of the thing. "I never try to rush men into marriage."

He chuckled. "Okay. Now you stick to that. I don't
like most people," he mused. "But I like you."

"I like you, too."

"In between hero worshipping me," he added outra-
geously.

She looked him over with a long sigh. "Can I help it
if you're the stuff dreams are made of?"

"Pull the other one. I'll see you tomorrow."

"That reminds me, there's a young man in juvenile detention that I'd like you to talk to for me," she said. "He's on a rocky path. Maybe you can turn him around."

He rolled his eyes upward. "Not again!"

"You know you don't mind," she chided. "I'll phone you from the office tomorrow."

"All right." He watched her get out of the Bronco. "Lock your doors."

His concern made her tingle. She grinned at him over her shoulder. "I always do. Thanks for supper."

"I enjoyed it."

"So did I." She wanted to, but she didn't look back as she unlocked the door. She was inside before she heard him drive off. She was sure that her feet didn't touch the floor for the rest of the night. And her dreams were sweet.

In the days and weeks that followed, Jessica and McCallum saw a lot of one another. He kissed her, but it was always absently, tenderly. He'd drawn back from the intensity of the kisses they'd shared the first night he took her out. Now, they talked about things. They discovered much that they had in common, and life took on a new beauty for Jessica.

Just when she thought things couldn't get any better, she walked into the Hip Hop Café and came face-to-face with a nightmare—Sam Jackson.

The sandy-haired man turned and looked at her with

cold, contemptuous eyes. He was the brother of the man who'd attacked her and who had later been killed. He was shorter and stockier, but the heavy facial features and small eyes were much the same.

"Hello, Jessica Larson," he said, blocking her path so that she was trapped between the wall and him. "I was passing through and thought I might look you up while I was in town. I wanted to see how my brother's murderer was getting along."

She clutched her purse in hands that trembled. She knew her face was white. Her eyes were huge as she looked at him with terror. He had been the most vocal person in court during the trial, making remarks about her and to her that still hurt.

"I didn't kill your brother. It wasn't my fault," she insisted.

"If you hadn't gone out there and meddled, it never would have happened," he accused. His voice, like his eyes, was full of hate. "You killed him, all right."

"He died in a car wreck," she reminded him with as much poise as she could manage. "It was not my fault that he attacked me!" She carefully kept her voice down so that she wouldn't be overheard.

"You went out there alone, knowing he'd be on his own because you'd tried to get his wife to leave him," he returned. "A woman who goes to a man's house by herself when he's alone is asking for it."

"I didn't know that he was alone!"

"You wanted him. That's why you convinced his wife to leave him."

The man's attitude hadn't changed, it had only intensified. He'd been unable from the beginning to believe his brother could have beaten not only his wife, but his little girl as well. To keep from accepting the truth, he'd blamed it all on Jessica. His brother had been the most repulsive human being she'd ever known. She looked at him levelly. "That's not true," she corrected. "And you know it. You won't admit it, but you know that your brother was on drugs and you know what he did because of it. You also know that I had nothing to do with his death."

"Like hell you didn't," he said with venom. "You had him arrested! That damned trial destroyed my family, humiliated us beyond belief. Then you just walked away. You walked off and forgot the tragedy you'd caused!"

Her whole body clenched at the remembered agony. "I felt for all of you," she argued. "I didn't want to hurt you, but nothing I did was strictly on my own behalf. I wanted to help his daughter, your niece! Didn't any of you think about her?"

He couldn't speak for a minute. "He never meant to hurt her. He said so. Anyway, she's all right," he muttered. "Kids get over things."

Her eyes looked straight into his. "No, they don't get over things like that. Even I never got over what your brother did to me. I paid and I'm still paying."

"Women like you are trash," he said scornfully. "And before I'm through, everyone around here is going to know it."

"What do you mean?"

He smiled. "I mean I'm going to stick around for a few days and let people know just what sort of social worker they've got here. Maybe during the last few years, some of them have forgotten…."

"If you try to start trouble—" she began.

"You'll what?" he asked smugly. "Sue me for defamation of character? Go ahead. It took everything we had in legal fees to defend my brother. I don't have any money. Sue me. You can't get blood out of a rock."

She tried to breathe normally, but couldn't. "How is Clarisse?" she asked, mentioning the daughter of the man who'd assaulted her so many years before.

"She's in college," he said, "working her way through."

"Is she all right?"

He shifted irritably. "I guess. We hear about her through a mutual cousin. She and her mother washed their hands of us years ago."

Jessica didn't say another word. She'd been planning to eat, but her appetite was gone.

"Excuse me, I have to get back to work," she said. She turned around and left the café. She hardly felt anything all the way to her office. She'd honestly thought the past was dead. Now here it was again, staring her in the face. She'd done nothing wrong, but it seemed that she was doomed to pay over and over again for a crime that had been committed against her, not by her.

It was a cruel wind that had blown Sam Jackson into town, she thought bitterly. But if he was only passing through, perhaps he wouldn't stay long. She'd stick close to the office for a couple of days, she decided, and not make a target of herself.

But that was easier said than done. Apparently Sam had found out where her office was, because he passed by it three times that day. The next morning, when Jessica went into work, it was to find him sitting in the Hip Hop Café where she usually had coffee. She went on to the office and asked Bess if she'd mind bringing her a coffee when she went across the street.

"Who is that fat man?" Bess asked when she came back. "Does he really know you?"

Jessica's heart stopped. "Did he ask you about me?"

"Oh, no," Bess said carelessly. She put a plastic cup of coffee in front of Jessica. "He didn't say anything to me, but he was talking to some other people about you." She hesitated, wondering if she should continue.

"Some people?" Jessica prompted.

"Sterling McCallum was one of them," the case-worker added slowly.

Jessica didn't have to ask if what the man had said

was derogatory. It was obvious from the expression on her face that it was.

"He said his brother died because of you," Bess continued reluctantly. "That you led him on and then threw him over after you'd gotten his wife out of the way."

Jessica sat down heavily. "I see. So I'm a femme fatale."

"Nobody who knows you would believe such a thing!" Bess scoffed. "He was a client, wasn't he? Or rather, his brother was. Honest to God, Jessica, I knew there had to be some reason why you always insist that Candy and Brenda go out on cases together instead of alone. His brother was the reason, wasn't he?"

Jessica nodded. "But that isn't how he's telling it. New people in the community might believe him, though," she added, trying not to remember that several old-timers still believed that Jessica had been running after the man, too.

"Tell him to get lost," the other woman said. "Or threaten to have him arrested for slander. I'll bet McCallum would do it for you. After all, you two are looking cozy these days."

"We're just friends," Jessica said with emphasis. "Nothing more. And Sterling might believe him. He's been away from Whitehorn for a long time, and he doesn't really know me very well." She didn't add that McCallum had such bad experiences in the past that it might be all too easy for him to believe what Sam Jackson was telling him. She was afraid of the damage that might be done to their fragile relationship.

"Don't worry," Bess was saying. "McCallum will give him his walking papers."

"Do you think so?" Jessica took a sip of her coffee. "We'd better get to work."

She half expected McCallum to come storming into the office demanding explanations. But he didn't. Nothing was said at all, by him or by anyone else. Life went on as usual, and by the end of the day, she'd relaxed. She'd overreacted to Sam's presence in Whitehorn. It would be all right. He was probably on his way out of town even now.

McCallum was drinking a beer. He hardly ever had anything even slightly alcoholic. His mother had taught him well what alcohol could do. Therefore, he was always on guard against overindulgence.

That being the case, it was only one beer. He was off duty and not on call. Before he'd met the newcomer in the café that morning, he might have taken Jessica to a movie. Now he felt sick inside. She'd never told him the things he'd learned from Sam Jackson.

Jessica was a pretty woman when she dressed up. She'd been interning at the social-services office, Sam Jackson had told him, when she'd gone out to see his brother Fred. Fred's wife had become jealous of the way Jessica was out there all the time, and she'd left him. Jessica teased and flirted with him, and then, when things got out of hand and the poor man was maddened with passion, she'd yelled rape and had him arrested. The man had hardly touched her. He'd gone to jail for attempted rape, got out on parole six months later and was killed in a horrible car wreck. His wife and child had been lost to him, he was disgraced and it was all Jessica's fault. Everybody believed her wild lies.

Sam Jackson was no fly-by-night con man. He'd been a respected councilman in Whitehorn for many years and was still known locally. McCallum had asked another old-timer, who'd verified that Jessica had had Jackson's brother arrested for sexual assault. It had been a closed hearing, very hushed up, and a bit of gossip was all that managed to escape the tight-lipped sheriff, Judd Hensley, and the attorneys and judge in the case. But people knew it was Jessica who had been involved, and the rumors had flown for weeks, even after Fred Jackson's family left town and he was sent to jail for attempted rape.

The old man had shaken his head as he recalled the incident. Women always said no when they meant yes, he assured McCallum, and several people thought that Jessica had only gotten what she'd asked for, going out to a man's house alone. Women had too goldarned much freedom, the old-timer said. If they'd never gotten the vote, life would have been better all around.

McCallum didn't hear the sexism in the remark; he was too outraged over what he'd learned about Jessica. So that shy, retiring pose was just that—an act. She'd played him for an absolute fool. No woman could be trusted. Hadn't he learned from his mother how treacherous they could be? His mother had smiled so sweetly when people came, infrequently, to the house. She'd lied with a straight face when a neighbor had asked questions about all the yelling and smashing of glass the night before. Nothing had happened except that she'd dropped a vase, she'd insisted, and she'd cried out because it startled her.

Actually, she'd been raving mad from too much alcohol and had been chasing her son around the house with an empty gin bottle. That was the night she'd broken his arm. She'd managed to convince the local doctor, the elderly practitioner who'd preceeded Jessica's father, that he'd slipped and fallen on a rain-wet porch. She'd tried to coax him to set it and say nothing out of loyalty to the family. But Sterling had told. His mother had hurt him. She'd lied deliberately about their home life. She'd pretended to love him, until she drank. And then she was like another person, a brutal and unfeeling one who only wanted to hurt him. He'd never trusted another woman since.

Until Jessica. She was the one exception. He'd grown close to her during their meetings, and he wanted her in every way there was. He valued her friendship, her company. But she'd lied to him, by omission. She hadn't told him the truth about her past.

There was one other truth Sam Jackson had imparted

to him, an even worse one. In the course of the trial, it had come out that the doctor who had examined Jessica found a blockage in her fallopian tubes that would make it difficult, if not impossible, for her to get pregnant.

She knew that Sterling was interested in her, that he would probably want children. Yet she'd made sure that she never told him that one terrible fact about herself. She could not give him a child. Yet she'd never stopped going out with him, and she knew that he was growing involved with her. It was a lie by omission, but still a lie. It was the one thing, he confessed to himself, that he could never forgive.

He was only grateful that he'd found her out in time, before he'd made an utter fool of himself.

Eight

Unfortunately, it was impossible for Jessica not to notice that McCallum's attitude toward her had changed since Sam Jackson's advent into town. He didn't call her that evening or the next day. And when she was contacted by the sheriff's office because the child of one of her client families—Keith Colson—was picked up for shoplifting, she wondered if he would have.

She went to the sheriff's office as quickly as she could. McCallum was there as arresting officer. He was polite and not hateful, but he was so distant that Jessica hardly knew what to say to him.

She sat down in a char beside the lanky boy in the interrogation room and laid her purse on the table. "Why did you do it, Keith?" she asked gently.

He shrugged and averted his eyes. "I don't know."

"You were caught in the act," she pressed, aware of McCallum standing quietly behind her, waiting. "The store owner saw you pick up several packages of cigarettes and stick them in your pockets. He said you even looked into the camera while you were doing it. You didn't try to hide what you were doing."

Keith moved restlessly in the chair. "I did it, okay? How about locking me up now?" he added to McCallum. "This time I wasn't an accomplice. This time I'm the—what do you call it?—the perpetrator. That means I do time, right? When are you going to lock me up?"

McCallum was scowling. Something wasn't right here. The boy looked hunted, afraid, but not because he'd been caught shoplifting. He'd waited patiently for McCallum to show up and arrest him, and he'd climbed into the back of the patrol car almost eagerly. There was one other disturbing thing: a fading bruise, a big one, was visible beside his eye.

"I can't do that yet," McCallum said. "We've called the juvenile authorities. You're under age, so you'll have to be turned over to them."

"Juvenile? Not *again!* But I wasn't an accomplice, you know I did it. I did it all by myself! I shouldn't have to go back home this time!"

McCallum hitched up his slacks and sat down on the edge of the table, facing the boy. "Why don't you tell me the truth?" he invited quietly. "I can't help you if I don't know what's going on."

Keith looked as if he wanted to say something, as if it was eating him up inside not to. But at the last minute, his eyes lowered and he shrugged.

"Nothing to tell," he said gruffly. He glanced at McCallum. "There's a chance that they might keep me, isn't there? At the juvenile hall, I mean?"

McCallum scowled. "No. You'll be sent home after they've done the paperwork and your hearing's scheduled."

Keith's face fell. He sighed and wouldn't say another word. McCallum could remember seeing that particular expression on a youngster's face only once before. It had been on his own face, the night the doctor set the arm his mother had broken. He had to get to the bottom of Keith's situation, and he knew he couldn't do that by talking to Keith or any of his family. There had to be another way, a better way. Perhaps he could talk to some people at Keith's school. Someone there might know more than he did and be able to shed some light on the situation for him.

Jessica went out to see Keith's father and grandmother. She'd hoped McCallum might offer to go with her, but he left as soon as Keith was delivered to the juvenile officer. It was all too obvious that he found Jessica's company distasteful, probably because Sam

Jackson had been filling his head full of half-truths. If he'd only come out and accuse her of something, she could defend herself. But how could she make any sort of defense against words that were left unspoken?

Terrance Colson was not surprised to hear that his son was in trouble with the law.

"I knew the boy was up to no good," he told Jessica blithely. "Takes after his mother, you know. She ran off with a salesman and dumped him on me and his grandmother years ago. Never wanted him in the first place." He sounded as if he felt the same way. "God knows I've done my best for him, but he never appreciates anything at all. He's always talking back, making trouble. I'm not surprised that he stole things, no, sir."

"Did you know that he smoked?" Jessica asked deliberately, curious because the boy's grandmother stayed conspicuously out of sight and never even came out to the porch, when Jessica knew she'd heard the truck drive up.

"Sure I knew he smoked," Terrance said evenly. "I won't give him money to throw away on cigarettes. That's probably why he stole them."

That was a lie. Jessica knew it was, because McCallum had offered the boy a cigarette in the sheriff's office and he'd refused it with a grimace. He'd said that he didn't like cigarettes, although he quickly corrected that and said that he just didn't want one at the moment. But there were no nicotine stains on his fingers, and he certainly didn't smell of tobacco.

"You tell them to send him home, now, as soon as they get finished with him," Terrance told Jessica firmly. "I got work to do around here and he's needed. They can't lock him up."

"They won't," she assured him. "But he won't tell us anything. Not even why he did it."

"Because he needed cigarettes, that's why," the man said unconvincingly.

Jessica understood why McCallum had been suspicious. The longer she talked to the boy's father, the more curious she became about the situation. She asked a few more questions, but he was as unforthcoming as Keith himself had been. Eventually, she got up to leave.

"I'd like to say hello to Mrs. Colson," she began.

"Oh, she's too busy to come out," he said with careful indifference. "I'll give her your regards, though."

"Yes. You do that." Jessica smiled and held out her hand deliberately. As Terrance reluctantly took it, she saw small bruises on his knuckles. He was righthanded. If he hit someone, it would be with the hand she was holding.

She didn't remark on the bruises. She left the porch, forming a theory that was very disturbing. She wished that she and McCallum were on better terms, because she was going to need his help. She was sorry she hadn't listened to him sooner. If she had, perhaps Keith wouldn't have another shoplifting charge on his record.

When she got back to her office, she called the sheriff's office and asked them to have McCallum drop by. Once, he would have stopped in the middle of whatever he was doing to oblige her. But today it was almost quitting time before he put in a belated appearance. And he didn't look happy about being summoned, either.

She had to pretend that it didn't matter, that she wasn't bothered that he was staring holes through her with those angry dark eyes. She forced a cool smile to her lips and invited him to sit down.

"I've had a long talk with Keith's father," she said at once. "He says that Keith smokes and that's why he took the cigarettes."

"Bull," he said curtly.

"I know. I didn't notice any nicotine stains on Keith's fingers. But I did notice some bruises on Terrance's knuckles and a fading bruise near Keith's eye," she added.

He lifted an eyebrow. "Observant, aren't you?" he asked with thinly veiled sarcasm. "You were the one who said there was nothing wrong at Keith's home, as I recall."

She sat back heavily in her chair. "Yes, I was. I should have listened to you. The thing is, what can we do about it? His father isn't going to admit that he's hitting him, and Keith is too loyal to tell anyone about it. I even thought about talking to old Mrs. Colson, but Terrance won't let me near her."

"Unless Keith volunteers the information, we have no case," McCallum replied. "The district attorney isn't likely to ask a judge to issue an arrest warrant on anyone's hunch."

She grimaced. "I know." She laced her fingers together. "Meanwhile, Keith's desperate to get away from home, even to the extent of landing himself in jail to accomplish it. He won't stop until he does."

"I know that."

"Then do something!" she insisted.

"What do you have in mind?"

She threw up her hands. "How do I know? I'm not in law enforcement."

His dark eyes narrowed accusingly on her face. "No. You're in social work. And you take your job very seriously, don't you?"

It was a pointed remark, unmistakable. She sat up straight, with her hands locked together on her cluttered desk, and stared at him levelly. "Go ahead," she invited. "Get it off your chest."

"All right," he said without raising his voice. "You can't have a child of your own."

She'd expected to be confronted with some of the old gossip, with anything except this. Her face paled. She couldn't even explain it to him. Her eyes fell.

The guilt told him all he needed to know. "Did you ever plan to tell me?" he asked icily. "Or wasn't it any of my business?"

She stared at the small print on a bottle of correction fluid until she had it memorized. "I thought…we weren't serious about each other, so it…wasn't necessary to tell you."

He didn't want her to know how serious he'd started to feel about her. It made him too vulnerable. He crossed one long leg over the other.

"And how about the court trial?" he added. "Weren't you going to mention anything about it, either?"

Her weary eyes lifted to his. "You must surely realize that Sam Jackson isn't anyone's idea of an unbiased observer. It was his brother. Naturally, he'd think it was all my fault."

"Wasn't it?" he asked coldly. "You did go out to the man's house all alone, didn't you?"

That remark was a slap in the face. She got to her feet, her eyes glittering. "I don't have to defend a decision I made years ago to you," she said coolly. "You have no right to accuse me of anything."

"I wasn't aware that I had," he returned. "Do you feel guilty about what happened to Jackson's brother?"

Her expression hardened to steel. "I have nothing to feel guilty about," she said with as much pride as she could manage. "Given the same circumstances, I'd do exactly what I did again and I'd take the consequences."

He scowled at her. "Including costing a man his family, subjecting him to public humiliation and eventually to what amounted to suicide?"

So that was what Sam had been telling people. That Jessica had driven the man to his death.

She sat back down. "If you care about people," she said quietly, "you believe them. If you don't, all the words in the world won't change anything. Sam should have been a lawyer. He really has a gift for influencing opinion. He's certainly tarred and feathered me in only two days."

"The truth usually comes out, doesn't it?" he countered.

She didn't flinch. "You don't know the truth. Not that it matters anymore." She was heartsick. She pulled her files toward her. "If you'll excuse me, Deputy McCallum, I've already got a day's work left to finish. I'll have another talk with Keith when the juvenile officers bring him back to the sheriff's office."

"You do that." He got up, furious because she wouldn't offer him any explanation, any apology for keeping him in the dark. "You might have told me the truth in the beginning," he added angrily.

She opened a file. "We all have our scars. Mine are such that it hurts to take them out and look at them." She lifted wounded dark eyes to his. "I can't ever have babies," she said stiffly. "Now you know. Ordinarily, you wouldn't have, because I never had any intention of letting our relationship go that far. You were the one who kept pushing your way into my life. If you had just let me alone…!" She stopped, biting her lower lip to stifle the painful words. She turned a sheet of paper over deftly. "Sam Jackson's brother got what he deserved, McCallum. And that's the last thing I'll ever say about it."

He stood watching her for a minute before he finally turned and went out. He walked aimlessly into the outer office. She was right. He was the one who'd pursued her, not the reverse. All the same, she might have told him the truth.

"Hi, McCallum," Bess called to him from her desk, smiling sweetly.

He paused on his way out and smiled back. "Hi, yourself."

She gave him a look that could have melted ice. "I guess you and Jessica are too thick for me to try my luck, hmm?" she asked with a mock sigh.

He lifted his chin and his dark eyes shimmered as he looked at her. "Jessica and I are friends," he said, refusing to admit that they were hardly even that anymore. "That's all."

"Well, in that case, why don't you come over for supper tonight and I'll feed you some of my homemade spaghetti?" she asked softly. "Then we can watch that new movie on cable. You know, the one with all the warnings on it?" she added suggestively.

She was pretty and young and obviously had no hang-ups about being a woman. He pursed his lips. It had been a long, dry spell, although something in him resisted dating a woman so close to Jessica. On the other hand, he told himself, Jessica had lied to him, and what was it to her if he dated one of her employees?

"What time?" he asked gruffly.

She brightened. "Six sharp. I live next door to Truman Haynes. You know where his house is, don't you?" He nodded. "Well, I rent his furnished cottage. It's very cozy, and old Truman goes to bed real early."

"Does he, now?" he mused.

She grinned. "Yes, indeed!"

"Then I'll see you at six." He winked and walked out, still feeling a twinge of guilt.

Bess stuck her head into Jessica's office just before she left. "McCallum said that you and he were just good friends, and you keep saying the same thing," she began, "so is it all right if I try my luck with him?"

Jessica was dumbfounded, but she was adept at hiding her deepest feelings. She forced a smile. "Why, of course."

Bess let out a sigh of relief. "Thank goodness! I invited him over for supper. I didn't want to step on your toes, but he is so sexy! Thanks, Jessica! See you tomorrow!"

She closed the door quickly, and a minute later, Jessica heard her go out. It was like a door closing on life itself. She hesitated just briefly before she turned her eyes back to the file she was working on. The print was so blurred that she could hardly read it.

Whitehorn was small and, as in most small towns, everyone knew immediately about McCallum's supper with Bess. They didn't know that nothing had happened, however, because Bess made enough innuendos to suggest that it had been the hottest date of her life. Jessica was hard-pressed not to snap at her employee, but she couldn't let anyone know how humiliating and painful the experience was to her. She had her pride, if nothing else.

Sam Jackson heard about the date and laughed heartily. Originally he'd planned to spend only one night in Whitehorn, but he was enjoying himself too much to leave in a rush. A week later, he was still in residence at the small motel and having breakfast every morning at the café across from Jessica's office.

Jessica was near breaking point. People were gossiping about her all over again. She became impatient with her caseworkers and even with clients, which was unlike her. She couldn't do anything about Sam Jackson, and certainly McCallum wasn't going to. He seemed to like the man. And he seemed to like Bess as well, because he began to stop by the office every day to take her to lunch.

"I'm leaving now," Bess said at noon on Friday. She hesitated, and from the corner of her eye, Jessica saw her looking at her in concern. No wonder since even to her own eyes she looked pale and drawn. In fact, she was hardly eating anything and was on the verge of moving out of town. Desperation had cost her the cool reason she'd always prided herself on.

"Have a nice lunch," she told Bess, refusing to look up because she knew Sterling McCallum was standing in the outer office, waiting.

Bess still hesitated. She felt so guilty she couldn't stand herself lately. It was painfully obvious how her boss

felt about Sterling McCallum. It was even more obvious
now that McCallum was taking Bess out. She hated being
caught between the two of them, and it was shocking to
see how Jessica was being affected by it. Bess had a few
bad moments remembering how she'd embroidered
those dates with McCallum to make everyone in the
office think they had a hot relationship going.

Jessica was unfailingly polite, but she treated Bess
like a stranger now. It was painful to have the old,
pleasant friendliness apparently gone for good. Jessica
never looked into her eyes. She treated her like a piece
of furniture, and it really hurt. Bess couldn't even blame
her. She asked for permission to go out with McCallum,
but she'd known even when Jessica gave it that the other
woman cared deeply about him. She was ashamed of
herself for putting her own infatuation with McCallum
over Jessica's feelings. Not that it had done her any
good. McCallum was fine company, and once he'd
kissed her with absent affection, but he couldn't have
made it more obvious that he enjoyed being with her
only in a casual way. On the other hand, when he looked
at Jessica there was real pain in his eyes.

"Can't I bring you back something?" Bess asked
abruptly. "Jessica, you look so—"

"I'm fine," Jessica said shortly. "I have a virus and
I've lost my appetite, that's all. Please go ahead."

Bess grimaced as she closed the door, and the concern
was still on her face when she joined McCallum.

He'd seen Jessica, too, in that brief time while her office door was open. He'd wanted to show her that he didn't care, that he could date other women with complete indifference to her feelings. But it was backfiring on him. He felt sick as he realized how humiliated she must be, to have him dating one of her own co-workers. It wasn't her fault that she couldn't bear a child, after all, and she was right—he'd never acted as if he had any kind of permanent relationship in mind for the two of them. He was still trying to find reasons to keep her at arm's length, he admitted finally. He was afraid to trust her, afraid of being hurt if he gave his heart completely. He'd believed Sam Jackson because he'd wanted to. But now, as he thought about it rationally, he wondered at his own gullibility. Was he really so desperate to have Jessica out of his life that he'd believe a total stranger, a biased total stranger, before he'd even ask Jessica for her version of what had happened?

Sam Jackson had been having lunch in the café, too, and stopped by McCallum's table to exchange pleasantries with him and Bess. Sheriff Hensley drove by in the patrol car and saw them in the window. Later that afternoon, he invited McCallum into his office and closed the door.

"I heard Sam Jackson's been in town six days," he said quietly. "What's his business here?"

"He's just passing through," McCallum said.

"And…?"

McCallum was puzzled. It wasn't like his boss to be

so interested in strangers who visited town. "And he's just passing the time of day as well, I guess."

Hensley folded his hands together on his desk and toyed with a paper clip. "He's the sort who holds grudges." He looked up. "I've heard some talk I don't like. It was a closed trial, but a lot of gossip got out anyway. Fred's wife and daughter left town as soon as the verdict was read, but Jessica had nowhere to go except here. Fred, of course, gave her a rough time of it."

"Maybe he had reason to," McCallum ventured curtly.

Hensley put the paper clip down deliberately. "You listen to me," he said coldly. "Jessica did nothing except try to help his wife and child. Fred was a cocaine addict. He liked to bring his friends home at night while his wife was working at the hospital. One night he was so high that he beat his daughter and she ran away. It was Jessica who took her in and comforted her. It was Jessica who made her mother face the fact that she was married to an addict and that she had to get help for them. Jessica was told—probably by your buddy Sam—that Fred had forced Clarisse, his daughter, to go back home with him. That's why she went out there that day. He attacked Jessica instead, and she barely got away in time."

McCallum didn't say a word. His complexion paled, just a little.

"For her pains, because the court trial was in the judge's chambers, and not publicized for Clarisse's sake, Jessica took the brunt of the gossip. All anyone heard was that Jessica had almost gotten raped. It was the talk of the town. Everywhere she went, thanks to Sam Jackson, she was pointed out and ridiculed as the girl who'd led poor Fred on and then yelled rape. She took it, for Clarisse's sake, until her mother could get another job and they could leave town while Fred was safely in jail."

"He didn't tell me that," McCallum said dully.

"Sam Jackson hated Jessica. He was on the city council. He had influence and he used it. But time passed and Sam left town. It didn't end there, however. Fred got out of jail in six months and came after Jessica. He was killed in a wreck, all right," the sheriff stated. "He was out for vengeance the day he was paroled and was chasing Jessica in his car, high as a March kite, until he ran off a cliff in the process. He would have killed her if he hadn't."

McCallum felt cold chills down his spine. He could picture the scene all too easily.

"Jessica survived," Hensley continued curtly, and McCallum barely registered the odd phrasing. "She held her head up, and those of us who knew the truth couldn't have admired her more. She's suffered enough. I didn't realize Sam Jackson was even in town until I happened to see him this morning, but he won't be here any longer. I'm going to give him a personal escort to the county line right now." He stood up, grabbing his hat. "And for what it's worth, I think you're petty to start dating Bess right under Jessica's nose, on top of everything else. She doesn't deserve that."

McCallum got to his feet, too. "I'd like a word with Jackson before you boot him out of town."

Hensley recognized the deputy's expression too well to agree to what McCallum was really suggesting.

"You believed him without questioning what he said," Hensley reminded him. "If there's fault, it's as much yours as his. You aren't to go near him."

McCallum's thin lips pressed together angrily. "He had no business coming here to spread more lies about her."

"You had no business listening to them," came the merciless reply. "Learn from the experience. There are always two sides to every story. You've got enough work to do. Why don't you go out there and act like a deputy sheriff?"

McCallum reached for his own hat. "I don't feel much like one right now," he said. "I've been a fool."

"Hard times teach hard lessons, but they stay with us. Jessica isn't judgmental, even if you are."

McCallum didn't say another word, but he had his reservations. He'd hurt her too much. He knew before he even asked that she might forgive him, but that she'd never forget the things he'd said to her.

Nine

Sam Jackson left town with the sheriff's car following him every inch of the way to the county line. He'd had to do some fast talking just to keep an irritated Hensley from arresting him for vagrancy. But his bitter hatred of Jessica hadn't abated, and he hoped he'd done her some damage. His poor brother, he told himself, had deserved some sort of revenge. Perhaps now he could rest in peace.

McCallum didn't go near Jessica's office, for fear that Bess might make another play for him and complicate things all over again. He did go to Jessica's house the next afternoon, hat in hand, to apologize.

She met him at the door in a pair of worn jeans and a T-shirt, her hair in a ponytail and her glasses perched on her nose. It was a beautiful day, and the Montana air sparkled. The world was in bloom, and the White-horn area had never been more beautiful under the wide blue sky.

"Yes?" Jessica asked politely, as if he were a stranger.

He felt uncomfortable. He wasn't used to making apologies. "I suppose you know why I'm here," he said stiffly.

She stripped off her gardening gloves. "It's about Keith, I guess," she replied matter-of-factly, without any attempt at dissembling.

He frowned. "No. We persuaded the authorities to keep Keith for a few days at the juvenile hall while we did some investigating. I haven't come about that."

"Oh." Her eyes held no expression at all. "Then what do you want?"

He propped one foot on the lowest step and stared at the spotless shine of his black boot. "I came to apologize."

"I can't imagine why."

He looked up in time to catch the bitterness that touched her face just for an instant. "What?"

"I'm a liar and a temptress and a murderess, according to Sam Jackson," she said heavily. "From what everyone says, you were hanging on to every word he said. So why should you want to apologize to me?"

He drew in a breath and shifted his hat from one hand to the other. "Hensley told me all of it."

"And that's why you're here." She sounded weary, resigned. "I might have known it wasn't because you came to your senses," she said without inflection in her voice. "You preferred Sam Jackson's version of the truth, even after I reminded you that he was biased."

"You told me a half-truth from the beginning!"

"Don't you raise your voice to me!" she said angrily, punching her glasses up onto her nose when they started to slip down. "I didn't want to remember it, can't you understand? I hate having to remember. Clarisse was the real victim, a lot more than I was. I just happened to be stupid enough to go out there alone, trying to protect her. And believe me, it wasn't to tempt Fred! The only thing I was thinking about was how to spare Clarisse any more anguish!"

"I know that now." He groaned silently. "Why didn't you tell me?"

"Why should you have expected me to?" she replied, puzzled. "I don't know very much about you, except that your mother drank and was cruel to you and that you had a very nasty time of it in foster care."

He hesitated, searching her eyes.

"You've told me very little about yourself," she said. "I only know bits and pieces, mostly what I've heard from other people. But you expected me to tell you things I haven't told anyone my whole life. Why should you expect something from me that you're not willing to give in return?"

That gave him food for thought. He ran a hand through his hair. "I don't suppose I should have."

"And it's all past history now," she added. "You're dating Bess. I don't trespass on other women's territory. Not ever. Bess even asked if I had anything going with you before she invited you to supper. I told her no," she added firmly.

There was a sudden faint flush high on his cheekbones, because he remembered telling Bess the same thing. But it wasn't true, then or now. "Listen—" he began.

"No, you listen. I appreciate the meals we had together and the help you gave me on cases. I hope we can work together amicably in the future. But as you have reason to know, I have nothing to offer a man on any permanent basis."

He moved closer, his eyes narrowed with concern. "Being barren isn't the end of the world," he said quietly.

She moved back and folded her arms over her chest, stopping him where he stood. "You thought so. You even said so," she reminded him.

His teeth ground together. "I was half out of my mind! It upset me that you could keep something so important to yourself. That was why I got uptight. It isn't that I couldn't learn to live with it…."

"But you don't have to. Nobody has to live with it except me," she said quietly. "I'm sure that Bess has no such drawbacks, and she has the advantage of being completely without inhibitions. She's sweet and young, and she adores you," she said through tight lips. "You're a very lucky man."

"Lucky," he echoed with growing bitterness.

"Now, if you'll excuse me," she said with a bright smile, pulling her gloves back on, "I have to finish weeding my garden. Thanks for stopping by."

"Just like that?" he burst out angrily. "I hadn't finished."

She brushed dirt off the palm of one glove. "What is there left to say?" she asked with calm curiosity.

He studied her impassive face. She had her emotions under impeccable control, but beneath the surface, he perceived pain and a deep wounding that wasn't likely to be assauged by any apology, however well meant. He was going to have to win back her trust and respect. That wasn't going to happen overnight. And he didn't expect her to make it easy for him.

He rammed his hat back onto his head. "Nothing, I guess," he agreed, nodding. "I said it all, one way or another, when I jumped down your throat without knowing the truth."

"Sam can be very convincing," she replied. She averted her face. "He turned the whole town against me for a while. You can't imagine how vicious the gossip was," she added involuntarily. "I still hate being talked about."

Jessica didn't add that he'd helped gossip along by dating Bess, so that his rejection of her was made public. But he knew that already. It must have added insult to injury to have his new romantic interest and Sam's renewed accusations being discussed at every lunch

counter in town. He understood now, as he hadn't
before, why she'd worried so much about being seen in
public with him.

"How about Jennifer?" she added suddenly, interrupt-
ing his gloomy thoughts. "Any news on her parents?"

"No luck yet," he replied. "But I think I may be on
to something with Keith."

"I hope so," she said. "I feel terrible that I didn't
suspect something before this."

"None of us is perfect, Jessica," he said, his voice
deep and slow and full of regret. His dark eyes searched
hers in silence, until she averted her own to ward off the
flash of electricity that persisted between the two of
them. "I'll let you know what I find out."

She nodded, but didn't reply. She just walked away
from him.

He talked to a school official about Keith, and discovered that the boy had been an excellent student until
about the time his father lost his job.

"He was never a problem," the counselor told him.
"But he let slip something once about his father liking
liquor a little too much when he was upset. Things
seemed to go badly for Terrance after his wife left, you
know. Losing his job must be the last straw."

"I'm sure it's unpleasant for him to have to depend
on public assistance," McCallum agreed. "But taking it
out on his child isn't the answer."

"People drink and lose control," the counselor said. "More and more of them, in these pressured economic times. They're usually sorry, too late. I'll try to talk to Keith again, if you like. But I can't promise anything. He's very loyal to his father."

"Most kids are," McCallum said curtly. He was remembering how he'd protected his brutal mother, right up until the night she'd broken his arm with the bottle. He'd made excuse after excuse for her behavior, just as Keith was probably doing now.

He contacted the juvenile officer and had a long conversation with him, but the man couldn't tell him any more than he already knew. Keith hadn't reached the end of his rope yet, and until he did, there was little anyone could do for him.

McCallum did get a break, a small one, in the abandoned-baby case. It seemed that a local midwife did remember hearing an old woman from out of town talk about delivering a child in a clandestine manner for a frightened young woman. It wasn't much to go on, but anything would help.

McCallum decided that it might be a good idea to share that tidbit with Jessica. He dreaded having to see Bess again, after the way he'd led her on.

But it turned out not to be the ordeal he'd expected. Bess was just coming back from the small kitchen with a cup of coffee when he walked into the office. She moved closer and grinned at him.

"Hi, stranger!" she said with a friendly smile. "How about some coffee?"

"Not just now, thanks." He smiled ruefully. "Bess, there's something I need to tell you."

"No, there isn't," she said with a sigh. "I'd already figured it all out, you know. I never meant to step on Jessica's toes, but I had a major crush on you that I had to get out of my system." She gave him a sheepish glance. "I didn't realize how painful it was going to be, trying to work here after I'd all but stabbed Jessica in the back. No one in the office will speak to me, and Jessica's very polite, but she isn't friendly like she used to be. Nothing is the same anymore."

"I'm sorry about that," he said, knowing it was as much his fault as hers.

She shrugged and moved a little closer. "Still friends?" she asked hesitantly.

"Of course," he replied gently. He bent and kissed her lightly on the cheek.

Jessica, who'd come into the outer office to ask Bess to make a phone call for her, got an eyeful of what looked like a tender scene and froze in place.

"Jessica," McCallum said roughly as he lifted his head and saw her.

Bess turned in time to watch her boss disappear back into her own office, her back straight and dignified.

"Well, that was probably the last straw," Bess groaned. "I was going to talk to her today and apologize."

"So was I," he replied. "She didn't deserve to be hurt any more, after what Sam Jackson did to her."

"I hope it's not too late to undo the damage," Bess added. Then she realized how false a picture she'd given everyone about her dates with McCallum, and she felt even worse. She'd embroidered them to make herself look like a femme fatale, because McCallum hadn't been at all loverlike. But her wild stories had backfired in the worst way. In admitting that she'd lied, she'd make herself look like a conceited idiot. Jessica was cool enough to her already. She hated the thought of compounding the problem with confessions of guilt.

"There's nothing to undo," McCallum replied innocently. "I did enjoy your cooking," he added gently.

"I'm glad." She hesitated nervously. She might as well tell him how she'd blown up their friendship, while there was still time. "McCallum, there's just one little thing—"

"Later," he said, patting her absently on the shoulder. "I've got to talk to Jessica about a case."

"Okay." She was glad of the reprieve. Not that she didn't still have to confess her half-truths to Jessica.

He knocked briefly on Jessica's door and walked in. She looked up from her paperwork. Nothing of her inner torment showed on her unlined face, and she even smiled pleasantly at him.

"Come in, Deputy," she invited. "What can I do for you?"

He closed the door and sat down across from her. "You can tell me that I haven't ruined everything between us," he said bluntly.

She looked at him with studied curiosity. "We're still friends," she assured him. "I don't hold grudges."

His jaw clenched. "You know that wasn't what I meant."

She put down the file she'd been reading and crossed her hands on it. "What can I do for you?" she asked pleasantly.

Her bland expression told him that he couldn't force his way back into her life. He couldn't make her want him, as she might have before things went wrong between them. She was going to draw back into her shell for protection, and it would take dynamite to get her out of it this time. He doubted if he could even get her to go out for a meal with him ever again, because she wouldn't want gossip about them to start up a second time. He'd never felt so helpless. Trust, once sacrificed, was hard to regain.

"What about Keith?" she asked. "I presume that's why you came?"

"Yes," he confirmed untruthfully. He sat back in the chair and told her about the talk he'd had with the school counselor. "But there's nothing we can do until I have some concrete reason to bring his father in for questioning. And Keith is holding out. The juvenile authorities can't dig anything out of him." He crossed his long legs.

"On the other hand, we may have a break in the Baby Jennifer case."

She started. It wasn't pleasant to hear him say that. She'd become so involved with the tiny infant that a part of her hoped the mother would never be found. She was shocked at her own wild thoughts.

"Have you?" she asked numbly.

"A midwife knows of an old woman who helped a frightened young woman give birth. I'm trying to track her down. It may be our first real lead to the mother."

"And if you find her, then what?" she asked intently. "She deserted her own little baby. What sort of mother would do that? Surely to God the courts won't want to give the child back to her!"

He'd never seen Jessica so visibly upset. He knew she'd allowed herself to become attached to the infant, but he hadn't realized to what extent until now.

"I'm sure it won't come to that," he said slowly. "Jessica, you aren't having any ideas about taking the baby yourself?" he added abruptly.

She glared at him. "What if I do? What can a court-appointed guardian do that I can't? I can manage free time to devote to a child, I make a good salary—"

"You can't offer her a settled, secure home with two parents," he said curtly. "This isn't the big city. Here in Whitehorn the judge will give prior consideration to a married couple, not a single parent."

"That's unfair!"

"I'm not arguing with that," he said. "I'm just telling you what to expect. You know the judges around here as well as I do—probably better, because you have more dealings with them. Most of them have pretty fixed ideas about family life."

"The world is changing."

"Not here, it isn't," he reminded her. "Here we're in a time capsule and nothing very much changes."

She started to argue again and stopped on a held breath. He was right. She might not like it, but she had to accept it. A single woman wasn't going to get custody of an abandoned baby in Whitehorn, Montana, no matter how great a character she had.

She faced the loss of little Jennifer with quiet desperation. Fate was unfair, she was thinking. Her whole life seemed to be one tragedy after another. She put her head in her hands and sighed wearily.

"She'll be better off in a settled home," he mumbled. He hated seeing her suffer. "You know she will."

She sat up again after a minute, resignation in her demeanor. "Well, I won't stop seeing her until they place her," she said doggedly.

"No one's asked you to."

She glared at him. "She wouldn't get to you, would she, Deputy?" she asked with bitter anger. "You can walk away from anyone and never look back. No one touches you."

"You did," he said gruffly.

"Oh, I'm sure Bess got a lot further than I did," she

said, her jealousy rising to the surface. "After all, she doesn't have any hang-ups and she thinks you're God's gift to women."

"You don't understand."

"I understand everything," she said bluntly. "You wanted to make sure that no one in town connected you with the object of so much scandal. Didn't you tell me once that you hated gossip because people talked about you so much when you were a boy? That's really why you started taking Bess out, isn't it? The fact that she was infatuated with you was just a bonus."

He scowled. "That wasn't why—"

She stood up, looking totally unapproachable. "Everyone knows now that Bess is your girlfriend. You're safe, McCallum," she added proudly. "No one is going to pair you off with me ever again. So let well enough alone, please."

He stood up, too, feeling frustrated and half-mad with restrained anger. "I'd been lied to one time too many," he said harshly. "Trust comes hard to me."

"It does to me, too," she replied in a restrained tone. "You betrayed mine by turning your back on me the first chance you got. You believed Sam instead of me. You wouldn't even come to me for an explanation."

His face tautened to steel. He had no defense. There simply was none.

"You needn't look so torn, McCallum. It doesn't matter anyway. We both know it was a flash in the pan and nothing more. You can't trust women and I'm not casual enough for affairs. Neither of us would have considered marriage. What was left?"

His dark eyes swept over her with quiet appreciation of her slender, graceful body. "I might have shown you, if you'd given me half a chance."

She lifted her chin. "I told you, I'm not the type for casual affairs."

"It wouldn't have been casual, or an affair," he returned. "I'm not a loner by choice. I'm by myself because I never found a woman I liked. Wanted, sure. But there has to be more to a relationship than a few nights in bed. I felt…more than desire for you."

"But not enough," she said, almost choking on the words. "Not nearly enough to make up for what I…am."

His face contracted. "For God's sake, you're a woman! Being barren doesn't change anything!"

She turned away. The pain was almost physical. "Please go," she said in a choked tone. She sat back down behind her desk with the air of an exhausted runner. She looked older, totally drained. "Please, just go."

He rammed his hands into his pockets and glared at her. "You won't give an inch. How do you expect to go through life in that sewn-up mental state? I made a mistake, okay? I'm not perfect. I don't walk around with a halo above my head. Why can't you forget?"

Her eyes were vulnerable for just an instant. "Because it hurt so much to have you turn away from me," she confessed huskily. "I'm not going to let you hurt me again."

His firm lips parted. "Jessica, we learn from our mistakes. That's what life is all about."

"Mistakes are what *my* life is all about," she said, laughing harshly. She rubbed her hand over her forehead. "And there are still things you don't know. I was a fool, McCallum, and it was your fault because you wouldn't take no for an answer. Why did you have to interfere? I was happy alone, I was resigned to it…."

"Why did you keep trying to take care of me?" he shot back.

She had to admit she'd gone out of her way in that respect. She glanced up and then quickly back down to her desk. "Temporary insanity," she pleaded. "You had no one, and neither did I. I wanted to be your friend."

"Friends forgive each other."

She gnawed her lower lip. She couldn't tell him that it was far more than friendship she'd wanted from him. But she had secrets, still, that she could never share with him. She couldn't tell him the rest, even now. His fling with Bess had spared her the fatal weakness of giving in to him, of yielding to a hopeless affair. If it had gone that far, she corrected. Because it was highly doubtful that it would have.

"What are you keeping back?" he asked. "What other dark skeletons are hiding in your closet?"

She pushed her hair back from her wan face. "None

that you need to know about, McCallum," she said, leaning back. She forced a smile. "Why don't you take Bess to lunch?"

"Bess and I are friends," he said. "That's all. And I've caused enough trouble around here. I understand that you're barely speaking to her. That's my fault, not hers."

She glared at him. "Bess is a professional who reports to me, and how I treat her is my business."

"I know that," he replied. "But she's feeling guilty enough. So am I."

Her eyebrows lifted. "About what?"

"Neither of us made your life any easier," he said. "I didn't know what happened to you. But even if you'd been all that Sam Jackson accused you of being, I had no right to subject you to even more gossip. Bess knows why I took her out. I could have caused her as much pain as I caused you. I have to live with that, too. Fortunately, she was no more serious than I was."

"That isn't what she told us," Jessica said through her teeth.

He stared at her with dawning horror. What stories had Bess told to produce such antagonism from Jessica, to make her look so outraged?

He scowled. "Jessica, nothing happened. We had a few meals together and I kissed her, once. That's all."

"It's gentlemanly of you to defend her," she said, stone faced. "But I'm not a child. You don't have to lie to protect her."

"I'm not lying!"

She pulled the file open and spread out the papers in it. "I'd like to know what you find out about that midwife," she said. "And about Keith, if the juvenile authorities get any results."

He stared at her for a long moment. "Tit for tat, Jessica?" he asked quietly. "I wouldn't believe you, so now you won't believe me?"

She met his eyes evenly. "That has nothing to do with it. I think you're being gallant, for Bess's sake," she replied. "It's kind of you, but unnecessary. Nothing you do with Bess or anyone else is my business."

He wouldn't have touched that line with a gloved hand. He stared at her for a long moment, searching for the right words. But he couldn't find any that would fit the situation.

He found plenty, however, when he closed Jessica's door and stood over Bess, who'd been waiting for him to finish.

"What did you tell her?" he asked bluntly.

She grimaced. "I embroidered it a little, to save face," she protested. "I thought we were going to be a hot item and it hurt my feelings that you didn't even want to kiss me. I'm sorry! I didn't know how hard Jessica was going to take it, or I'd never have made up those terrible lies about us."

He grimaced. "How terrible?"

She flushed. She couldn't, she just couldn't, admit that! "I'll tell her the truth," she promised. "I'll tell her all of it, honest I will. Please don't be mad."

"Mad." He shook his head, walking toward the door. "I must be mad," he said to himself, "to have painted myself into this sort of corner. Or maybe I just have a talent for creating my own self-destruction."

He kept walking.

Ten

The last words McCallum spoke to Bess might have been prophetic. He was thinking about Jessica when he shouldn't have been, and he walked into a convenience store outside town not noticing the ominous silence in the place and the frightened look on the young female clerk's face.

It seemed to happen in slow motion. A man in a faded denim jacket turned with a revolver in his hand. As McCallum reached for his own gun, the man fired. There was an impact, as if he'd been hit with a fist on his upper arm. It spun him backwards. A fraction of a second later, he heard the loud pop, like a firecracker going off. In that one long minute while he tried to react, the perpetrator forgot his quarry—Tammie Jane, the terrified young clerk—and ran out the door like a wild man.

"You've been shot! Oh, my goodness, what shall I do?" Tammie Jane burst out. She ran to McCallum, her own danger forgotten in her concern for him.

"It's not so bad," he said, gritting his teeth as he pulled out a handkerchief to stem the surging, rhythmic flow of blood. "Nothing broken, at least, but it looks as if the bullet may have…clipped an artery." He wound the handkerchief tighter and put pressure over the wound despite the pain it caused. "Are you all right?"

"Sure! He came in and asked for some cigarettes, and when I turned to get them, he pulled out that gun. Gosh, I was scared! He'd just told me to empty the cash register when you walked in."

"I walked in on it like a raw recruit," he added ruefully. "My God, I don't know where my mind was. I didn't even get off a shot."

"You're losing a lot of blood. I'd better call for an ambulance—"

"No need. I'll call the dispatcher on my radio." He made his way out to his patrol car, weaving a little. He was losing blood at a rapid rate and his head was spinning. He raised the dispatcher, gave his location and succinctly outlined the situation, adding a terse description of the suspect and asking for an all-points bulletin.

"Stay put. We'll send the ambulance," the dispatcher said, and signed off. The radio blared with sudden activity as she first called an ambulance and then broadcast a BOLO—a "be on the lookout for" bulletin—on the municipal frequency.

The clerk came out of the store with a hand towel and passed it to McCallum. His handkerchief was already soaked.

"I don't know how to make a tourniquet, but I'll try if you'll tell me how," Tammie Jane volunteered worriedly. Blood from his wound was pooling on the pavement, as McCallum was holding his arm outside the car.

He leaned back against the seat, his hand still pressing hard on the wound. "Thanks, but the ambulance will be here any minute. I can hear the siren."

It was fortunate that Whitehorn was a small town. Barely two minutes later, the ambulance sped up and two paramedics got out, assessed the situation and efficiently loaded a dazed McCallum onto a stretcher and into the ambulance.

He was still conscious when they got to the hospital, but weak from loss of blood. They had him stabilized and the blood flow stemmed before they pulled up at the emergency-room entrance.

He grinned sheepishly as they unloaded him and rolled him into the hospital. "Hell of a thing to happen to a law-enforcement officer. I got caught with my eyes closed, I guess."

"Thank your lucky stars he was a bad shot," one of them said with an answering smile. "That's only a flesh wound, but it hit an artery. You'd have bled to death if you'd taken your time about calling us."

"I'm beginning to believe it."

They wheeled him into a cubicle and called for the resident physician who was covering the emergency room.

Jessica had had a long morning, and her calendar was full of return calls to make. McCallum had shaken her pretty badly about Baby Jennifer. She hadn't been facing facts at all while she was spinning cozy daydreams about herself and the baby together in her cozy cottage.

Now she was looking into a cold, lonely future with nothing except old age at the end of it. From the bright, flaming promise of her good times with McCallum, all that was left were ashes.

She took off her glasses and rubbed her tired eyes. She'd just about given up wearing the contact lenses now that she wasn't seeing McCallum anymore. She didn't care how she looked, except in a business sense. She dressed for the job, but there was no reason to dress up for a man now. She couldn't remember ever in her life feeling so low, and there had been plenty of heartaches before this one. It seemed as if nothing would go right for her.

The telephone in the outer office rang noisily, but Jessica paid it very little attention. She was halfheartedly going through her calendar when Bess suddenly opened Jessica's office door and came in, pale and unsettled.

"Sterling McCallum's been shot," she blurted out, and was immediately sorry when she saw the impact the words had on Jessica, who stumbled to her feet, aghast.

"Shot?" she echoed helplessly. "McCallum? Is he all right?"

"That was Sandy. She's a friend of mine who works at the hospital. She just went on duty. She said he was in the recovery room when she got to the hospital. Apparently it happened a couple of hours ago. Goodness, wouldn't you think *someone* would have called us before now? Or that it would have been on the radio? Oh, what am I saying? We don't even listen to the local station."

"Does Sandy know how bad he is?" Jessica asked, shaken.

"She didn't take time to find out. She called me first." She didn't add that it was because Sandy thought, like most people did, that McCallum and Bess were a couple. "All she knew was that he'd been shot and had just come out of emergency surgery."

"Cancel my afternoon appointments," Jessica said as she gathered up her purse. "I'll finish this paperwork when I get back, but I don't know when that will be."

"Do you want me to drive you?" Bess offered.

Jessica was fumbling in her purse for the keys to her truck. "No. I can drive myself."

Bess got in front of her in time to prevent her from rushing out the door. "I lied about Sterling and me," she said bluntly, flushing. "It wasn't true. He didn't want anything to do with me and I was piqued, so I made up a lot of stuff. Don't blame him. He didn't even know I did it."

Jessica hesitated. She wanted to believe it, oh, so much! But did she dare?

"Honest," Bess said, and her eyes met Jessica's evenly, with no trace of subterfuge. "Nothing happened."

"Thanks," Jessica said, and forced a smile. Then she was out the door, running. If he died… But she wouldn't think about that. She had to remember that to stay calm, and that they hadn't said he was in critical condition. She had to believe that he would be all right.

It seemed to take forever to get to the hospital, and when she did, she couldn't find a parking space. She had to drive around, wasting precious time, until someone left the small parking area reserved for visitors. There had been a flu outbreak and the hospital was unusually crowded.

She ran, breathless, into the emergency room. She paused at the desk to ask the clerk where McCallum was.

"Deputy McCallum is in the recovery room three doors down," the clerk told her. "Wait, you can't go in there…!"

Jessica got past a nurse who tried to stop her and pushed into the room, stopping at the sight of a pale, drawn McCallum lying flat on his back, his chest bare and a thick bandage wrapped around his upper arm. There were tubes leading to both forearms, blood being pumped through one and some sort of clear liquid through the other.

The medical team looked up, surprised at Jessica's sudden entrance and white face.

"Are you a relative?" one of them—probably the doctor—asked.

"No," McCallum said drowsily.

"Yes," Jessica said, at the same time.

The man blinked.

"He hasn't got anyone else to look after him," Jessica said stubbornly, moving to McCallum's side. She put her hand over one of his on the table.

"I don't need looking after," he muttered, hating having Jessica see him in such a vulnerable position. He was groggy from the aftereffects of the anesthetic they'd given him while they removed the bullet and repaired the damage it had done.

"Well, actually, you do, for twenty-four hours at least," the doctor replied with a grin. "We're going to admit him overnight," he told Jessica. "He's lost a lot of blood and he's weak. We want to pump some antibiotics into him, too, to prevent infection in that wound. He's going to have a sore arm and some fever for a few days."

"And he can't work, right?" she prompted.

McCallum muttered something.

"Right," the doctor agreed.

"I'll stay with him tonight in case he needs anything," Jessica volunteered.

McCallum turned his head and looked up at her with narrow, drowsy dark eyes. "Sackcloth and ashes, is it?" he asked in a rough approximation of his usual forceful tones.

"I'm not doing penance," she countered. "I'm helping out a friend."

For the first time, his eyes focused enough to allow him to see her face clearly. She was shaken, and there was genuine fear in her eyes when she looked at him. Probably someone had mentioned the shooting without telling her that it was relatively minor. She looked as if she'd expected to find him dead or shot to pieces.

"I'm all right," he told her. "I've been shot before, and worse than this. It's nothing."

"Nothing!" she scoffed.

"A little bitty flesh wound," he agreed.

"Torn ligament, severed artery that we had to sew up, extensive loss of blood…" the doctor was saying.

"Compared to the last time I was shot, it's nothing," McCallum insisted drowsily. "God, what did you give me? I can't keep my eyes open."

"No need to," the doctor agreed, patting him gently on his good shoulder. "You rest now, Deputy. You'll sleep for a while and then you'll have the great-grand-father of a painful arm. But we can give you something to counteract that."

"Don't need any more…painkillers." He yawned and his eyes closed. "Go home, Jessica. I don't need you, either."

"Yes, you do," she said stubbornly. She looked around her, realizing how crazy she'd been to push her way in. She flushed. "Sorry about this," she said, backing toward the door. "I didn't know how badly he was hurt. I was afraid it was a lot worse than this."

"It's all right," the doctor said gently. He smiled. "We'll take him to his room and you can sit with him there, if you like. He'll be fine."

She nodded gratefully, clutching her purse like a life jacket. She slipped out of the room and went to sit down heavily in a chair in the waiting room. Her heart was still racing and she felt sick. Just that quickly, McCallum could have been dead. She'd forgotten how uncertain life was, how risky his job was. Now she was face-to-face with her own insecurities and she was handling them badly.

When they wheeled him to a semiprivate room, she went along. The other half of the room was temporarily empty, so she wouldn't have to contend with another patient and a roomful of visitors. That was a relief.

She noticed that there was a telephone, and when McCallum had been settled properly and the medical team had left, she dialed her office and told Candy his condition and that she wouldn't be back, before asking to be transferred to Bess.

"Can I bring you anything?" Bess offered.

"No, thank you. I'm fine." She didn't want Bess here. She wanted McCallum all to herself, with no intrusions.

It was selfish, but she'd had a bad fright. She wanted time to reassure herself that he was all right, that he wasn't going to die.

"Then call us if you need us," Bess said. "I talked to Sandy again and told her the truth, so she won't, well, say anything to you about me and Sterling McCallum. I'm glad he's going to be okay, Jessica."

"So am I," she agreed. She hung up and pulled a chair near the bed. She'd noticed a strange look from one of the nurses earlier. That had probably been Bess's friend.

McCallum was sleeping now, his expression clear of its usual scowl. He looked younger, vulnerable. She grimaced as she looked at his poor arm and thought how painful it must have been. She didn't even know if they'd caught the man who'd shot him. Presumably they were combing the area for him.

A few minutes later, Sheriff Hensley and one of the other deputies stopped by the room to see him. Hensley had gone by McCallum's house to feed Mack and get McCallum a change of clothing. The shirt he'd been wearing earlier was torn and covered in blood. McCallum was still sleeping off the anesthesia.

"Have you caught the man who did it?" Jessica asked.

Hensley shook his head irritably. "Not yet. But we will," he said gruffly. "I wouldn't have had this happen for the world. McCallum's a good man. On the salary the job pays, we don't get a lot of men of his caliber."

Jessica had never questioned a man of McCallum's

education and background working in such a notoriously low-paying job. "I wonder why he does a lot of things," she mused, watching the still, quiet face of the unconscious man. "He's very secretive."

"So are you."

She grimaced. "Well, everyone's entitled to a skeleton or two," she reminded him.

He shrugged. "Plenty of us have them. Tell him I fed his dog, and brought those things by for him. I'll be back tomorrow. Are they going to try to keep him overnight?"

"Yes," she said definitely. "I'll stay with him. He won't leave unless he knocks me out."

"Harris here can stay with you if you think you'll need him," Hensley said with a rare smile.

Jessica glanced at the pleasant young deputy. "Thanks, but the doctor has this big hypodermic syringe…."

"Good point." Hensley took another look at McCallum, who was sleeping peacefully. "Tell him we're on the trail of his assailant. We're pretty sure who it is, from the description. We're watching the suspect's grandmother's house. It's the one place he's sure to run when he thinks it's safe."

Jessica nodded. "That's one advantage of small towns, isn't it?" she mused. "At least we generally know who the scoundrels are and where to find them."

"It makes police work a little easier. The police are helping us. McCallum's well liked."

"Yes." She looked up. "Thanks for getting Sam Jackson off my back."

He smiled. "Neighbors help each other. Maybe you'll do me a favor one day."

"You just ask."

"Well, a loaf of that homemade raisin bread wouldn't exactly insult me," he volunteered.

"When I get McCallum out of here, raisin bread will be my first priority," she promised him.

The way she worded it amused him, but it shocked her that she should feel proprietorial about McCallum, who'd given her no rights over him at all. She'd simply walked in and taken charge, and he wasn't going to like it. But she knew what he'd do if she left—go home this very night and back to work in the morning. He didn't believe in mollycoddling himself. No, she couldn't leave. She had to keep him here overnight and then make sure that he rested as the doctor had told him to. But how was she going to accomplish that?

She was still worrying about the problem when he woke up, after dark, and winced when he tried to stretch. They had a hospital gown on him, and the touch of the soft cotton fabric seemed to irritate him. He tried to pull it off.

Jessica got up and restrained his hand. They still had tubes in him, the steady drips going at a lazy speed.

"No, you mustn't," she said gently, bending over him.

His eyes opened. He stared at her and then looked around and frowned. "I'm still here?"

She nodded. "They want you to stay until tomorrow. You're very weak and they haven't finished the transfusion."

He let out a long, drowsy breath. "I feel terrible. What have they done to me?"

"They stitched you up, I think," she said. "Then they gave you something to make you rest."

He looked up at her again, puzzled. "What are you doing here? It's dark."

"I'm staying tonight, too," she said flatly. Her eyes dared him to argue with her.

"What for?"

"In case you need anything. Especially in case you try to leave," she added. "You're staying right there, McCallum. If you make one move to get up, I'll call the nurse and she'll call the doctor, and they'll fill you so full of painkillers that you'll sleep until Sunday."

He glared at her. "Threats," he said, "will not affect me."

"These aren't threats," she replied calmly. "I asked the doctor, and he said he'd be glad to knock you out anytime I asked him to if you tried to leave."

"Damn!" He lifted both hands and glared at the needles. "How did I get into this mess?"

"You let a man shoot you," she reminded him.

"I didn't let him," he said gruffly. "I walked in without looking while he was trying to rob the store. I didn't even see the gun until the bullet hit me. A police special, no less!" he added furiously. "It was a .38. No wonder it did so much damage!"

"I'm very glad he can't shoot straight," she said.

"Yes. So am I. He was scared—that's probably why he missed any vital areas. He fired wildly." His eyes closed and his face tightened as he moved. "I hope I get five minutes alone with him when they catch him. Have you heard from Hensley?"

"He and Deputy Harris came by to see you while you were asleep. They think they know who it was. They're staking out one of his relative's houses."

"Good."

"Didn't you know the place was being robbed? Wasn't that why you went in?" she persisted.

"I went in because I wanted a cup of coffee," he said with a rueful smile. "I don't think I'll ever want another one after this. Or if I do, I'll make it at home."

"I could ask the nurse if you can have one now," she offered.

"No, thanks. I'll manage." He hesitated. "Do they have a male nurse on this floor?"

"Yes."

"Could you ask him to step in here, please?"

She didn't have to ask why. She went out to find the nurse and sent him in. She waited until she saw him come out again before she rejoined McCallum.

"Damned tubes and poles and machines," he was

muttering. He looked exhausted, lying there among the paraphernalia around the bed. He turned his head and looked at her, seeing the lines in her face, the lack of makeup, the pallor. "Go home."

"I won't," she said firmly. She sat back down in the chair beside his bed. "I'll leave the hospital when you do. Not before."

His eyebrows lifted. "Have I asked you to be responsible for me?" he asked irritably.

"Somebody has to," she told him. "You don't have anybody else."

"Hensley would sit with me if I asked him, or any of the deputies."

"But you wouldn't ask them," she replied. "And the minute I walk out the door, you'll discharge yourself and go home."

"I need to go home. What about Mack?" He groaned. "He'll have to go without his supper."

"Sheriff Hensley has already fed him. He also brought you a change of clothing."

That seemed to relax him. "Nice of him," he commented. "Who'll feed Mack tomorrow morning and let him out?"

"I guess we'll have to ask the sheriff to go again. I'd offer, but that dog doesn't like women. I don't really want to go into your house when you aren't there. He growls at me."

"Your cat growls at me. It didn't stop me from going to your house."

"Meriwether couldn't do too much damage to you. But Mack is a big dog with very sharp teeth."

His eyes searched hers. "Afraid of him?"

"I guess maybe I'm afraid of being chewed up," she said evasively.

"Okay. Hand me the phone."

She did, and helped him push the right buttons. He phoned Hensley and thanked him, then asked him about feeding Mack in the morning. Hensley already knew McCallum kept a spare key in his desk and had used it once already. He readily agreed to take care of Mack.

"That's a load off my mind," McCallum said when he finished and lay back against the pillows. He flexed his shoulder and then frowned. "Do I smell something?"

As he said that, the door opened and a nurse came in bearing two trays. "Dinnertime," she said cheerfully, arranging them on the table. "I brought one for you, too, Miss Larson," she added. "You haven't even had coffee since you've been here."

"That's so nice of you!" Jessica said. "Thank you!"

"It's our pleasure. Make sure he eats," she added to Jessica on her way out. "He'll need all the protein he can get to help replenish that lost blood."

"I'll do that," Jessica promised.

She lifted the tops off the dishes on one tray while McCallum made terrible faces.

"I hate liver," he told her. "I'm not eating it."

She didn't answer him. She cut the meat into small,

bite-sized pieces and proceeded to present them at his lips. He glared at her, but after a minute of stubborn resistance, opened his mouth and let her put the morsels in, one at a time.

"Outrageous, treating a grown man like this," he muttered. But she noticed that he didn't refuse to eat, as he easily could have. In fact, he didn't lodge a single protest even when she followed the liver with vegetables and, finally, vanilla pudding.

It was intimate, doing this for him. She hadn't considered her actions at all, but now she realized that they could be misconstrued by a large number of people, starting with McCallum. She was acting like a lovesick idiot. What must he have thought when she came bursting into the recovery room where he was lying, forcing her way into his life like this?

She fed him the last of the pudding and, with a worried look, moved the tray to the other table.

"Now eat your own dinner before it gets cold," he insisted. "If you're determined to stay here all night, you need something to keep you going."

"I'm not really hungry…."

"Neither was I," he said with a cutting smile. "But *I* didn't have any choice. Now do you pick up that fork, or do I climb out of this bed and pick it up for you?"

His hand went to the sheet. With a resigned sigh, she uncovered her own plate and took it, and her fork, back to her chair. She didn't like liver any more than he did, but she ate it. At least it was filling.

He watched her until she cleared her plate and finished the last drop of her coffee. "Wasn't that good?" he taunted.

"I hate liver," she muttered.

"So do I, but that didn't save me." He grinned at her. "Turnabout is fair play."

She sighed, standing to replace her plate on the tray. She hadn't touched her pudding.

"Aren't you going to eat that?" he asked.

"I like chocolate," she muttered. "I hate vanilla."

"I don't." His eyes twinkled. "Want to feed it to me?"

Her blush was caused more by the silky soft tone of his voice than by the words. She couldn't help it.

"If you like," she said hesitantly.

"Come on, then."

She got the pudding and approached the bed. But when she started to open the lid, he caught her hand and tugged until she bent forward.

"Sterling!" she protested weakly.

"Humor me," he whispered, reaching up to cup her chin in his lean hand and pull her face down. "I'm a sick man. I need pampering."

"But—"

"I want to kiss you," he whispered at her lips. "You can't imagine how much. Just a little closer, Jessie. Just another inch…"

She sighed against his hard mouth as she moved that

tiny distance and let her lips cover his. He made a soft sound and, despite the tubes attached to his arm, his hand snaked behind her head to increase the pressure of his mouth. She stiffened, but it was already too late to save herself. The warm insistence of the kiss worked its way through all her doubts, fears and reservations and touched her very soul. She sighed and gave in to the need to reassure herself that he was alive. Her own mouth opened without coyness and she felt the shock that ran through him before he groaned and deepened the kiss.

The sound of a tray rattling outside the room brought her head up. He looked somber and his eyes were narrow and hot.

"Coward," he taunted.

Her lips felt swollen. She pulled gently back from him and stood up, her knees threatening to give way. He had an effect on her body that no other man ever had. There were so many reasons why she shouldn't allow this feeling between them to grow. But other than disappointment, there was no other emotion left in her at the moment. That, and a raging pleasure that turned quickly to frustration.

Eleven

The nurse came in to remove the dishes, and somehow Jessica managed to look calm and pleasant. But inside, her whole being was churning with sensation. She looked at Sterling and her mouth tingled in memory.

She was wondering how she was going to manage the situation, but then the doctor came in on his rounds and ordered a sedative for the patient. It was administered at once, and McCallum glowered as the nurse finished checking his vital signs and the technicians came back to get some samples they needed for the lab. It was fifteen minutes before they left him alone with Jessica. And by then, the shot was beginning to take effect.

"Hell of a thing, the way they treat people here," he

murmured as his eyelids began to droop. "I wanted to talk to you."

"You can talk tomorrow. Now go to sleep. You'll feel better in the morning."

"Think so?" he asked drowsily. "I'm not sure about that."

He shifted and a long sigh passed his lips. Only seconds later, he was dozing. Jessica settled in her chair with a new paperback she'd tucked into her purse after a brief stop at the bookstore on her way to lunch. She must have had some sort of premonition, she mused. And unlike McCallum, she didn't have to worry about her pet. Meriwether had plenty of water and cat food waiting for him, and a litter box when he needed it. He might be lonely, but he wouldn't need looking after. She opened the book.

But the book wasn't half as interesting as McCallum. She finally put it aside and sat looking at him, wishing that her life had been different, that she had something to offer such a man. He was a delight to her eyes, to her mind, her heart, her body. She couldn't have imagined anyone more perfect. He liked her, that was obvious, and he was attracted to her. But for his own sake, she had to stop things from progressing any further than liking. Her own weakness was going to be her worst enemy, especially while he was briefly vulnerable and needed her. She had to be sure that she didn't let his depleted state go to her head. Above all, she had to keep her longings under control.

Eventually, she tried to sleep. But the night was long and uncomfortable as she tried to curl up in the padded chair. In the morning, McCallum was awake before she was, and she opened her eyes to find him propped up in bed watching her.

"You don't snore," he commented with a gentle smile.

"Neither do you," she returned.

"Fortunate for us both, isn't it?"

She sat up, winced and stretched. Her hair had come down in the night and it fell around her shoulders in a thick cloud. She pushed it back from her face and readjusted her glasses.

"Why don't you wear your contact lenses?" he asked curiously. "And before you fly at me, I don't mean you look better with them or anything. I just wondered why you'd stopped putting them in."

She stood up. "It didn't seem worth the effort anymore," she said. "And they're not as comfortable as these." She touched the big frames with her forefinger. She smiled. "And they're a lot of trouble. Maybe I'm just lazy."

He smiled. "Not you, Jessie."

"How do you feel?"

"Sore." He moved his shoulder with a groan. "It's going to be a few days before I feel like much, I guess."

"Good! That means you won't try to go back to work!"

He glowered at her. "I didn't say that."

"But you meant it, didn't you?" she pressed with a wicked grin.

He laid his head back against the pillow. "I guess so." He studied her possessively. "Are you coming home with me?"

Her heart jumped up into her throat. "What?"

"How do you expect to keep me at home if you don't?" he asked persuasively. "Left on my own, I'm sure I'd go right back to the office."

There was a hint of cunning in his eyes, and she didn't trust the innocent expression on his face. He had something in mind, and she didn't want to explore any possibilities just now.

"You could promise not to," she offered.

"I could lie, too."

"I have a job," she protested.

"Today is Friday. Tomorrow is Saturday. What do you do that someone else can't do as well for one day?"

"Well, nothing, really," she said. She hesitated. "People might talk…."

"Who gives a damn?" he said flatly. "We've both weathered our share of gossip. To hell with it. Come home with me. I need you."

Those three words made her whole body tingle with delight. She stared at him with darkening eyes, with a faint flush on her cheekbones that betrayed how much the statement affected her.

"I need you," he repeated quietly.

"All right."

"Just like that?"

She smiled. "Just like that. But only for today," she added.

His eyebrows rose. "Why, Jessica, did you think I was inviting you to spend the night with me?"

She glowered back. "You stop that. I'm just going to take care of you."

He beamed. "What a delightful prospect."

Her jaws tightened. "You know what I mean, and it isn't that!"

"I know what I wish you meant," he teased softly.

"You're going to be a handful, aren't you?" she asked with resignation.

"I'll try not to cause you a lot of trouble." He studied her long and intently. "Besides, how difficult can it be?" He indicated his shoulder. "I'm not in any shape for what you're most concerned about. Long, intimate sessions on my sofa will have to wait until I'm properly fit again, Jessica," he added in a soft, wicked tone. "Sorry if that disappoints you."

She turned away to keep him from seeing the flush on her cheeks. "Well, if you're going to leave today, I'd better see if the doctor agrees that you can. I'll go and check at the nurses' station."

"You tell them that even if he says I can't, I'm going home," he informed her.

She didn't argue. It wouldn't really do any good.

By noon, they'd discharged him, and Jessica, after stopping by her house to change clothes and feed her cat, drove him to his house. It disturbed her a little to have her pickup truck sitting in his driveway, but there wasn't a lot she could do about it. He wasn't able to cook or clean, and there was no one else she could ask to do it—except possibly Bess, and that was out of the question.

She hesitated when he unlocked the door and Mack growled at the sight of her.

"Stop that," McCallum snapped at the dog.

Mack stopped at once, eagerly greeting his master.

McCallum petted him and motioned Jessica into the house before he dropped heavily into his favorite armchair.

"It's good to be home," he remarked.

"How about something to eat?" she asked. "You didn't stay long enough to have lunch."

"I wasn't hungry then. There's a pizza in the freezer and some bacon and eggs in the fridge."

"Any flour?"

He glared at her. "What the hell would I want with flour?"

She threw up her hands. It wasn't a question she should have asked a bachelor who liked frozen pizza.

"So much for hopes of quiche," she said half to herself as she put down her purse and walked toward the kitchen.

"Real men don't eat quiche," he called after her.

"You would if you had any flour," she muttered. "But I guess it's going to be bacon and eggs."

"We could order a pizza from the place downtown."

"I don't want pizza. And you need something healthy."

"I won't eat tofu and bean sprouts."

She was searching through the refrigerator and vegetable bins. There were three potatoes and a frozen pizza, four eggs of doubtful age, a slice of moldy bacon and a loaf of green bread.

"Don't you ever clean things out in here?" she called.

He shrugged, then winced as the movement hurt his shoulder. "When I get time," he told her.

She came back and reached for her purse. "Please don't try to go to work while I'm gone."

"Where, exactly, are you going?"

"To get some provisions," she said. "Some *edible* provisions. You couldn't feed a dedicated buzzard on what's in your kitchen."

He chuckled and reached for his wallet. He handed her a twenty-dollar bill. "All right. If you're determined, go spend that."

"I'll need to stop by my office, too."

"Whatever."

She hesitated in the doorway, indecision on her face.

"If you'd rather I sent Bess over—"

"Bess was a pleasant companion," he replied. "She was never anything more, regardless of what she might have told you."

"Okay." She went out and closed the door behind her.

She stopped by the office just long enough to delegate some chores and answer everyone's concerns about McCallum. Bess was interested, but not overly so, and she smiled reassuringly at Jessica before she told her to wish him well.

After that, Jessica went shopping. When she got back to McCallum's house, he was sprawled on the sofa in his sock feet with a can of beer in his hand, watching a movie.

"What did you buy?" he asked as she carried two plastic sacks into the kitchen.

"Everything you were out of." She handed him back two dollars and some change.

He glanced at the grocery bags. "What are you going to cook me?"

"Country-fried cubed steak, gravy, biscuits and mashed potatoes."

"Feel my pulse. I think I've just died and gone to heaven. Did I hear you right? I haven't had that since it was a special at the café last month."

"I hope it's something you like."

"'Like' doesn't begin to describe how I feel about it. Try 'overwhelmed with delight.' But to answer your question, yes, I like it."

"It's loaded with cholesterol and calories," she added, "but I can cut down on the grease."

"Not on my account." He chuckled. "I love unwholesome food."

She prepared the meal in between glimpses of the movie he was watching. It was a thriller, an old police drama set back in the thirties, and she enjoyed it as much as he did. Later, they ate in front of the television and watched a nature special about the rain forest.

"That's a good omen," he said when they'd finished and she was collecting the plates.

"What is?"

"We like the same television programs. Not to mention the same food."

"Most people like nature specials."

"One woman I dated only watched wrestling," he commented.

She stacked the plates and picked them up. "I don't want to hear about your other dates."

"Why not?" he asked calculatingly. "I thought you only wanted to be friends with me."

She stopped, searching for words. But she couldn't quite find the right ones, so she beat it back to the kitchen and busied herself washing dishes. Mack sat near her on the floor, watching her without hostility. It was the first time since she'd been in the house that he didn't growl at her.

She put away the dishcloth and cleaned up the kitchen. There was enough food left for McCallum to have for supper. She put it on a platter and covered it, so that he could heat it up later.

He'd turned off the television when she came back into the living room. He was lying full length on the sofa with his eyes closed, but he opened them when he heard her step. His dark eyes slid up and down her body, over the simple blue dress that clung to her slender body. The expression in them made her pulse race.

"I should…go home." Her voice faltered.

He didn't say a word. His hand went to his shirt and slowly, sensually, unfastened it. He moved it aside, giving her a provocative view of his broad, hair-roughened chest.

"I have things to do," she continued. She couldn't quite drag her eyes away from those hard, bronzed muscles.

He held out his good arm, watching her in a silence that promised pleasures beyond description.

She knew the risks. She'd known them from the first time she saw him. Up until now, they'd weighed against her. But the realization of how close he'd come to death shifted the scales.

She went to him, letting him draw her down against him, so that she was stretched out beside him on the long sofa, pressed close against his hard, warm body.

"Relax," he said gently, easing her onto her back and grimacing as he moved to loom over her. "I'm not stupid enough to start something I can't finish."

"Are you sure?" she asked a little worriedly, because the minute her hips tilted into his, she felt the instant response of his body.

"Not really." He groaned and laughed softly in the same breath, shifting her away slightly. "But let's pretend that I am. I like you in this dress, Jessie. It fits in all the right places. But I don't like the way it fastens.

Too damned many buttons and hooks in back…. Ah, that's better."

"McCallum!" she cried as the bodice began to slip. She made a grab for it, but his fingers intercepted the wild movement.

"What are you afraid of?" he murmured softly, smiling down at her. "It won't hurt."

She bit her lower lip. "I…can't let you look at me," she said, lowering her eyes to the hard throbbing of his pulse in his neck.

He frowned. "Now, or ever?" he asked with a patience he didn't feel.

"E-ever," she clarified. She pulled the bodice closer. "Let me up, please, I want to…McCallum!"

Even with a bullet wound, he was stronger and quicker than she was. The dress was suddenly around her waist, and he was looking at her body in the wispy nylon bra with its strategically placed lace. But it wasn't her breasts that had his attention.

She closed her eyes and shivered with pain. "I tried to stop you," she said harshly, biting back tears. "Now, will you let me go!"

"My God." The way he spoke was reverent. But there was no revulsion, either in the words or in his face. There was only pain, for what she must have suffered.

"Oh, please," she whispered, humiliated.

"There's no need to look like that," he said quietly. "Lie still. I'm going to take you out of this dress."

"No...!"

He caught her flailing hand and brought it to his mouth, kissing the palm gently. His dark eyes met her wild ones. "You need to be made love to," he said softly. "More than you realize. You're not hideous, Jessica. The scars aren't that bad."

She fought tears and lost. They fell, hot and profuse, pouring down her cheeks. Her hand relaxed its hold on her dress and she lay still, letting him smooth away it and her half-slip and pantyhose until she lay there in only her briefs and bra.

He bent and she felt with wonder the touch of his mouth as it traced the thin white lines from her breasts down her belly to where they intersected just below her naval.

His big, lean hand held her hip while he caressed her with his mouth, his thumb edging under the lace of the briefs to touch her almost, but not quite, intimately. She caught her breath at the sensations he was teaching her and arched involuntarily toward the pleasure.

"You crazy woman," he breathed as he lifted his head and looked down into her dazed, hungry eyes. "Why didn't you tell me?"

"I thought... They're so ugly."

He only smiled. He bent and his mouth brushed lazily over hers, parting her lips, teasing, tasting. And while he held her in thrall, his hand went behind her to find the single catch. He freed it and lazily tugged the bra away from her firm, high breasts.

She didn't protest. His eyes on her gave her the purest delight she'd ever known. She gazed up at him with rapt wonder while he looked and looked until her nipples grew hard and began to ache.

Then, finally, he began to touch them, and she shivered with sensations she'd never known. Her lips parted as she tried to catch her breath.

He chuckled with appreciation and triumph. "All that time wasted," he murmured. "They're very sensitive, aren't they?" he added when she jerked at the faint brush of his fingertips. He took the hardness between his thumb and forefinger and pressed it gently, and she cried out. But it wasn't because he was hurting her. She was responsive to a shocking degree. That embarrassed her, because he was watching her like a hawk, and she tried to push his hand away.

"Shh," he whispered gently. "Don't fight it. This is for you. But when you're a little more confident, I'm going to let you do the same thing to me and watch how it excites me. I'm just as susceptible as you are, just as hungry."

"You're…watching me," she got out.

"Oh, yes," he agreed quietly. "Can you imagine how it makes me feel, to see the pleasure my touch gives you?" His fingers contracted and she shivered. "My God, I couldn't get my head through a doorway right now, do you know that? You make me feel like ten times the man I am."

He bent and put his mouth where his fingers had

been. She whimpered at first and pushed against him frantically.

He lifted his head and looked into her eyes, seeing the fear.

"Tell me," he said softly.

"He…bit me there," she managed hoarsely.

He scowled. His eyes went to her body and found the tiny scars. His expression hardened to steel as he touched them lightly.

"I won't bite you," he said deeply. "I promise you, it won't hurt. Can you trust me enough to let me put my mouth on you here?"

She searched his face. He wasn't a cruel man. She knew already that he was protective toward her. She let herself relax into the soft cushions of the sofa and her hands dropped to his shoulders, lingering there, tremulous.

"Good," he whispered. He bent again, slowly. This time it was his tongue she felt, soothing and warm, and then the whispery press of his lips moving on soft skin. The sensations were a little frightening, because they seemed to come out of nowhere and cause reactions not only in her breasts, but much lower.

His hand slid down her body and slowly trespassed under the elastic.

She should protest this, she should tell him to…stop!

He felt her nails bite into him, heard her moans grow, felt her body tauten almost to pain.

He lifted his head and stopped. Her face was gloriously flushed, her eyes shy and hungry and frustrated. She looked at him with wonder.

"Your body is capable of more pleasure than you know," he said gently. "I won't hurt you."

She arched back faintly, involuntarily asking for more, but he moved away. He wasn't touching her now. He was propped just over her, watching her face, her body.

"Why did you stop?" she whispered helplessly.

"Because it's like shooting fish in a barrel," he said simply. "You've just discovered passion for the first time in your life. I want to be sure that it's me, and not just new sensations, that are motivating you. The next step isn't so easy to pull back from, Jessie," he added solemnly. "And I don't know if I can make love completely with my shoulder in this fix."

She blinked, as if she hadn't actually realized how involved they were becoming.

His eyes dropped to her taut breasts and down her long, elegant legs before they moved back up to meet her shy gaze. He didn't smile even then. "I didn't really understand before," he said. "You were involved in the crash that killed Fred, weren't you? You were damaged internally in the wreck."

She nodded. "Fred was released because of a technicality six months after he went to prison. He blamed me for all his trouble, so he got drunk and laid in wait for me one night when I was working late. He chased me and ran me off the road. I was hurt. But he was killed." She shivered, remembering that nightmare ride. "They had to remove an ovary and one of my Fallopian tubes. Even before the accident the doctors thought I'd be unlikely to get pregnant, and now... Well, it would be a long shot."

His face didn't change, his expression didn't waver. He didn't say a word.

She grimaced. "You need children, Sterling," she said in a raw whisper, her eyes mirroring the pain in the words. "A wife who loves you, and a home." Her gaze fell to his broad, bare chest and her hands itched to touch him.

"And you think that puts you out of the running?" he asked.

"Doesn't it?"

His fingers pressed down gently over her belly, and his hand was so big that it almost covered her stomach completely. "You're empty here," he said, holding her gaze. "But I'm empty here."

His hand moved to his chest, where his heart was, before it dropped back down beside her to support him. "I've never been loved," he said flatly. "I've been wanted, for various reasons. But my life has been conspicuously lacking in anyone who wanted to look after me."

"Bess did," Jessica recalled painfully.

He touched her mouth with his fingertips. "Bess is young and unsettled and looking for something that she hasn't found yet. I'm fond of her. But I never felt desire for her. It's hard to explain," he added with a humorless laugh, "but for me, desire and friendship don't usually go together."

She searched his face. "They didn't, with Bess?"

"That's right. Not with *Bess*."

He emphasized the name, looking at her with more than idle curiosity.

"With…anyone else?"

He nodded.

Obviously, she was going to have to drag it out of him, but she had to know. "With…me?" she asked, throwing caution to the winds.

"Yes," he said quietly. "With you."

She didn't know how to answer him. Her body felt hot all over at the look he was giving her. She'd never known passion until now, and it was overwhelming her. She wanted him, desired him, ached for him. She wanted to solve all the mysteries with him. The inhibitions she'd always felt before were conspicuously absent.

She felt her breasts tightening as she stared at the hair-matted expanse of his muscular chest.

"Are you surprised that you can feel desire, after all you've been through?" he asked gently.

"Yes."

"But then, strong emotions can overcome fear, can't they?" He bent, nuzzling his face against her bare breasts, savoring the softness of her skin against his. "Jessie, if my arm didn't throb like blazing hell, I'd have you right here," he breathed. "I ache all over from wanting you."

"So do I," she confessed. She slid her arms around his neck and pressed her body completely against his, shivering a little when she felt the extent of his arousal.

He felt her stiffen and his hands were gentle at her back. "Lie still," he whispered. "It's all right. You're in no danger at all."

"I never dreamed that I could feel like this," she whispered into his throat, where her face was pressed. "That I could want like this." Her breasts moved against the thick hair that covered his chest and she moaned at the sensations she felt.

His lean hand slipped to the base of her spine and one long leg moved, so that he could draw her intimately close, letting her feel him in an embrace they'd never shared.

Her intake of breath was audible and she moaned harshly. So did he, pushing against her roughly for one long, exquisite minute until he came to his senses and rolled away from her. He got unsteadily to his feet with a rough groan.

"Good God, I'm losing it!" he growled. He made it to the window and stared out, gripping the sash. He fought to breathe, straining against the throbbing pain of his need for her.

She lay still for a minute, catching her own breath, before she sat up and quickly got back into her clothes. Her long hair fell all around her shoulders in tangles, but she couldn't find the pins he'd removed that had held it in place.

He turned finally and stared at her with his hands deep in his pockets. He was pale and his shoulder hurt.

"They're in my pocket," he told her, smiling gently at her flush. "Embarrassed, now that we've come to our senses?"

She lifted her eyes to his. "No," she said. "I don't really think I can be embarrassed with you. I—" she smiled gently "—I loved what you did to me."

Twelve

For a minute, he didn't seem to breathe at all. Then his eyes began to soften and a faint smile tugged at the corners of his mouth.

"In that case," he said, "we might do it again from time to time."

She smiled, too. "Yes."

He couldn't remember when he'd felt so warm and safe and happy. Just looking at Jessica produced those feelings. Touching her made him feel whole.

"I should go," she said reluctantly. "Meriwether will need his food and water changed, and I have other chores to do."

He thought about how the house was going to feel when she left, and it wasn't very pleasant. He'd been alone all his life and he was used to it. It had never bothered him before, but suddenly, it did. He frowned as he studied her, wondering at the depth of his feelings, at his need to be near her all the time. Once he would have fought that, but something had rearranged his priorities…perhaps getting shot.

"Okay," he said after a minute. "Let me feed Mack and we'll go."

Her heart flew up. "*We'll* go…. You're coming home with me?"

He nodded.

Her lips parted as she looked at him and realized that he didn't want to be separated from her any more than she wanted to be apart from him.

"Did you think it was one-sided?" he asked, moving toward her. "Didn't it occur to you that in order for something to be this explosive, it has to be shared?"

Her expression mirrored her sense of wonder. So did his. He pulled her against him, wincing a little when the movement tugged at his stitches, and bent his head. He kissed her with slow, aching hunger, feeling her instant response with delight.

"If I go home with you, people will really talk about us," he whispered against her mouth. "Aren't you worried?"

"No," she said with a smile. "Kiss me…."

He did, thoroughly, and she returned it with the same hunger. After a minute, he had to step back from her. His chest rose and fell heavily as he searched her eyes.

"Do you have a double bed?" he asked.

"Yes." She flushed and then laughed at her own embarrassment. That part of their relationship was something she'd have to adjust to, but she wasn't too worried about being able to accomplish it.

He touched her mouth with aching tenderness. "I was teasing," he chided. "I can't stay, as much as I want to. But I'll stay until bedtime."

"You could sleep on the sofa," she offered.

"I know that. I'll have one of the guys pick me up and drive me home. I don't want you alone on the roads late at night." He gently touched her cheek, which was flushed at his concern for her. "It's going to be rough. I don't want to be apart from you anymore, even at night. Especially at night," he said with a rough laugh.

"Yes, I know. I feel the same way." With her fingertips, she traced his thick eyebrows and then his closed eyelids, his cheeks, his mouth. "It's…unexpected. What are we going to do now?"

"Get married as soon as we can," he said simply. He smiled reluctantly at her expression. "Don't faint on me, Jessie."

"But you don't want to get married," she protested. "You said you never wanted to."

"Honey, do you think we could live together in Whitehorn without raising eyebrows?" he asked gently.

He smiled. "Besides that, when my shoulder heals, I'm going to have you. It's inevitable. We want each other too badly to abstain for much longer. Let's do this thing properly, by the book."

She traced a pattern in the thick tangle of hair on his broad chest. All her dreams hadn't prepared her for the reality of this. She could hardly believe it. "Marriage," she whispered with aching hunger. She lifted her eyes to his lean, hard face. "Someone of my own," she added involuntarily.

"There's that, too. Belonging to another person." He brought her hand to his lips. His teeth nipped the soft palm and she laughed. The glitter in his eyes grew. "You've never had a man, have you? Except for that one bad experience, you're untouched."

"Not anymore," she murmured demurely. "I've been all but ravished today."

He chuckled. "If you think that was ravishment, you've got a lot to learn."

She searched his eyes and sadness overlaid her joy. "It's a lovely dream. But it isn't realistic. It will matter to you one day, not being able to have a child of your own."

He touched her mouth and his face became as serious as hers. "Jessie, if you could have a child with another man, but not with me, would you marry him?"

She looked confused for a minute. "Well, no," she said. "Why?"

"Because I lo...because I care for you," she corrected.

He pulled her close. "You're not getting away with that," he said. "Tell me. Say the words."

She gnawed at her lower lip, hesitating.

"All the way, Jessie," he coaxed. "Say it."

"You won't," she said accusingly.

"I don't need to," he asserted. "If sex was all I wanted from you, I could have seduced you long ago. If it isn't just for the sake of sex, what other reason would I have for wanting to marry you?"

He hadn't said it, but she looked at him and realized with a start that he was telling her he loved her with everything except words. He couldn't bear to be parted from her, he wanted to marry her even though she couldn't give him a child....

"Of course I love you," she whispered softly. "I've loved you from the first time I saw you, but I never dared to hope—"

The last of the sentence was lost under the soft, slow crush of his mouth on her lips. He drew her close and kissed her with tenderness and passion, savoring her mouth until he had to lift his head to breathe. Yes, it was there, in her eyes, in her face; she loved him, all right. He began to smile and couldn't stop.

"You're surprisingly conventional," she mused, staring at him with loving eyes.

"Depressingly so, in some ways. I want the trimmings. I've never had much tradition in my life, but it starts now. We get engaged, then we get married, in

church, and you wear a white gown and a veil for me
to lift up when I kiss you."

She sighed. "It sounds lovely."

"It's probably Victorian." He chuckled. "Abstinence
until the event and all. But a little tradition can be beautiful. All that separates people from animals, I read
once, is a sense of nobility and honor. These days people
want instant satisfaction. They don't believe in self-
denial or self-sacrifice, or patience. I do. Those old
virtues had worth."

"Indeed they did. I'm just as old-fashioned at heart as
you are," she said gently. "I believe in forever, Sterling."

He drew her close and held her, hard. "So do I. We'll
have differences, but if we compromise and work at it,
we can have a long and happy life together." He kissed
her forehead with breathless tenderness, grimacing,
because holding her pulled the stitches and made his
arm throb. But it was a sweet pain, for all that.

"My job…" she began.

He smoothed her hair away from her face. "I work.
You work. We won't have to worry about someone
staying home with a child."

Her face contorted.

"Don't," he said gently. He scowled with concern.
"Don't. We'll be happy together, I promise you we will.
It's all right."

She had to fight down the tears. She pressed against
him and closed her eyes. She would never stop regret-

ting her condition. But perhaps Sterling was right. There would be compensations. First and foremost would be having this man love her as she loved him.

It took several weeks for McCallum's arm to heal completely, but they announced their wedding plans almost immediately. No one was really surprised, especially not Bess.

"When I saw how you looked at him that day, it didn't surprise me when I heard the news," Bess said with a grin. "I'm happy for both of you, honestly. I hope I get that lucky someday."

"Thanks," Jessica said warmly.

The office staff gave her an engagement party, complete with necessary household goods to start out—even though she'd accumulated a lot of her own. It was the thought that counted, and theirs were warm and pleasant.

An invitation to the wedding of Mary Jo and Dugin was forthcoming. It would take place in late June, about a month before Jessica and Sterling's. They decided to go together.

Meanwhile, another problem cropped up quite unexpectedly.

Keith Colson had finally done something that landed him in the purview of the county sheriff and not the juvenile authorities. He held up a small car dealership out in the country.

The pistol he used was not loaded, and he didn't

even run. They picked him up not far away, walking down a lonely highway with his sack of money. He even smiled at the sheriff's deputy—not McCallum—who arrested him.

He was brought into the sheriff's office for questioning, with new marks on his face.

This time McCallum wasn't willing to listen to evasions. He sat Keith down in the interrogation room and leaned forward intently.

"I've been too involved in my own life lately to see what was going on around me," he told Keith. "I meant to check on you again when the juvenile authorities released you, but I got shot and I've been pretty well slowed down. Now, however, I'm going to get to the root of this problem before you end up in federal prison." He looked the boy straight in the eye. "Your father is beating you." He watched Keith's eyes dilate. "And probably hitting your grandmother, too. You're going to tell me right now exactly what he's done to you."

Keith gaped at him. He couldn't find words. He shifted nervously in the chair. "Listen, it's not that—"

"Loyalty is stupid after a certain point," McCallum said shortly. "I was loyal to my mother, but when she broke my arm, I decided that my own survival was more important than the family's dark secret."

Keith's expression changed. "Your mother broke your arm?"

McCallum nodded curtly. "She was an alcoholic.

She couldn't admit that she had a problem and she couldn't stop. It just got worse, until finally I realized that if she really cared about me, she'd have done something to help herself. She wouldn't, so I had to. I had her arrested. It was painful and there was a lot of gossip. Afterwards, I had no place to go, so I got shuffled around the county, to whichever farm needed an extra hand in exchange for bed and board. She died of a heart attack in jail when I was in my early teens. I had a hell of a life. But even then it was better than having to fend her off when she came at me with bottles or knives or whatever weapon she could lay her hand on."

Keith seemed to grow taller. He let out a long sigh and rubbed the arms of the old wooden chair. "You know all about it then."

"Living with an alcoholic, you mean? Yes, I know all about it. So you won't fool me anymore. You might as well come clean. Protecting your father isn't worth getting a criminal record that will follow you all your life. You can't run away from the problem by getting thrown in jail, son. In fact, you'll find people worse than your father there."

Keith leaned forward and dangled his hands between his knees. "He says it's because he lost his job and nobody else will hire him, at his age. But I don't believe it anymore. He hits my grandma, you see. Mostly he hits her, and I can't stand that, so I try to stop him. But he hits me when I interfere. Last time I landed a couple of shots, but he's bigger than I am. Whenever he sobers up, he says he'll quit. He always says he'll quit, that it will get better." He shook his head and smiled with a cynicism beyond his years. "Only it doesn't. And I'm scared he'll really hurt Grandma one day. But if I left, she could, too. She only stays to try and make some sort of home for me, and cook and clean for us. She can't talk to him. Neither can I. He just doesn't hear us."

"He'll hear me," McCallum said, rising.

"What will you do?" Keith asked miserably.

"I'll pick him up for assault and battery, and you'll sign a warrant," he told the boy. "He may go to jail, but they'll help him and he'll dry out. Meanwhile, we'll place you in a foster home. Your grandmother is too old to look out for you, and she's got a sister in Montana who'd enjoy her company."

"Miss Larson told you, I guess," he mused, smiling sheepishly.

"Yes. Jessica and I are getting married."

"I heard. She's a nice lady."

"I think so."

"You won't hurt my dad?"

"Of course not."

The boy got to his feet. "There's this robbery charge...."

"I'll talk to Bill Murray," McCallum said. "When he knows the circumstances, he won't press charges. The money was all recovered and he knows the gun wasn't loaded. He's a kind man, and not vindictive."

"I'll write him a note and tell him how sorry I am. I

didn't want to do it, but I couldn't turn Dad in," he added, pleading for understanding.

McCallum clapped him on the back. "Son, life is full of things we can't do that we have to do. You'll learn that the hard part is living with them afterward. Come on. Let's go see the magistrate."

A warrant was sworn out and signed, and McCallum went to serve it. He felt sorry for Terrance Colson, but sorrier for the boy and his grandmother, who were practically being held hostage by the man.

He found Terrance sitting on his front porch, and obviously not expecting company, since he had a bottle of whiskey in one hand.

"What the hell do you want?" he demanded belligerently. "If it's that damned boy again, you can lock him up and throw away the key. I've had it with him!"

"He's had it with you, too, Terrance," McCallum replied, coming up onto the porch. "This is a warrant for your arrest, for assault and battery. Keith signed it."

"A…what?"

He stumbled to his feet, only to have McCallum grab him and whirl him around to face the wall, pinning him there while he cuffed him efficiently.

"You can't do this to me," Terrance yelled, adding a few choice profanities to emphasize his anger.

The door opened timidly and little Mrs. Colson peered out. Her eyes were red and there was bad bruises on one cheek and around her mouth.

"Are you...gonna take him off?" she asked McCallum.

He had to fight for control at the sight of the bruises on that small, withered face. "Yes, ma'am," he said quietly. "He won't be home for a while. The very least that will happen to him is that he'll be sent off to dry out."

She slumped against the door facing. "Oh, thank God," she breathed, her voice choked. Tears streamed down her face. "Oh, thank God. I've always been too weak and afraid to fight back, and Terrance takes after his daddy—"

Terrance glared at her. "You shut your mouth...!"

McCallum jerked him forward. "Let's go," he said tersely. "Mrs. Colson, Jessica will be out this afternoon to talk to you when I tell her what's happened. I have an idea about where we can place Keith, but we'll talk about that later. Are you all right? Do you need me to take you to the doctor?"

"No, thank you, sir," she replied. "If you'll just carry him off, that's all I need. That's all I need, yes, sir."

Terrance yelled wild, drunken threats at her, which made McCallum even angrier. But he was a trained law-enforcement officer, and didn't allow his fury to show. He was polite to Terrance, easing him into the patrol car with a minimum of fuss. He called goodbye to Mrs. Colson and took Terrance off to jail.

Later, Jessica went with Sterling and Keith to talk to Mrs. Colson.

"This is short notice, but I called Maris Wyler before

I came out here. She needs a good hand out at her ranch, and when I explained the circumstances, she said she'd be happy to have Keith if he wanted to come."

"Do I ever!" Keith interjected. "Imagine, Gram, a real ranch! I'll learn cowboying!"

"If that's what you want, Son," Mrs. Colson said gently. "Heaven knows, it's about time you had some pleasure in life. I know how you love animals. I reckon you'll fit right in on a ranch. It's very nice of Maris to let you come."

"She's a good woman. She'll take care of Keith, and he'll be somewhere he's really needed," McCallum told the old woman. "He and I have had a long talk about it. The judge has offered to let him plead to a lesser charge in exchange for a probationary sentence in Maris's custody. He'll have a chance to change his whole life and get back on the right track. She's even going to arrange for the homebound teacher to come out and give him his lessons so he won't have to go to school and face the inevitable taunting of the other students."

Mrs. Colson just nodded. "That would be best, Keith," she told her grandson. "I tried to help you as much as I could, but I couldn't fight your father when he was drinking."

"It's all right, Gram," Keith said gently. "You did all you could. I wish you could stay."

"I do, too, but this is your father's house and I could never stay here again."

"Yeah, neither could I," Keith replied. "It wouldn't ever be the same again, even if he does dry out. He talked about moving, and maybe he will. But I won't go with him. The way he's gotten, I'm not sure he wants to change. I'm not sure he can."

"The state will give him the opportunity to try," McCallum told them. "But the rest is up to him. If you want to see him, I can arrange it."

Keith actually shivered. "No, thanks," he said with a laugh. "When can I go and see this lady who says she'll take me in?"

"Right now, I guess," McCallum said with a grin. "We'll take Jessica with us, in case we need backup."

Keith frowned. "This sounds serious."

"Maris is a character," he replied. "But she's fair and she has a kind heart. You'll do fine. Just don't get on the wrong side of her."

"What he means," Jessica said, with a pointed glance at McCallum, "is that Maris is a strong and capable woman who can run a ranch all by herself."

McCallum started to open his mouth.

"You can shut up," Jessica interrupted him deftly. "And you'd better not swagger in front of Maris, or she'll cut you off at the ankles. She isn't the forgiving, long-suffering angel of mercy that I am."

"And not half as modest." McCallum grinned.

Jessica made a face at him, but love gleamed out of her soft brown eyes—and his, too. They had a hard time separating work from their private lives, but they managed it. They lived in each others' pockets, except at night. The whole town looked at them with kind indulgence, because they were so obviously in love that it touched people's hearts.

Even old Mrs. Colson smiled at the way they played. It took her back fifty years to her own girlhood and her late husband.

"Well, we'd better be on our way. I'll drive you to the bus station when you're packed and ready to leave," McCallum told her. "And if there's anything we can do, please let us know."

"All I need is to leave here," she replied, touching her swollen cheek gingerly. "Thank you for trying to help me, Son," she told Keith. "You were the only reason I stayed at all. I was scared of what he'd do to you if I left."

"I kept trying to find ways to get out," Keith confessed, "so that you could leave. But they kept sending me home again."

"Well, nobody's perfect, not even the criminal-justice system," McCallum said, tongue-in-cheek.

They left Mrs. Colson with an ice bag on her cheek and drove to the No Bull Ranch. Maris Wyler came out to meet them.

She was tall and lean, very tan from working outdoors, her long golden hair pulled back into a ponytail. She wore jeans and boots and a faded long-sleeved shirt, but she looked oddly elegant even in that rig.

"You're Keith. I'm Maris," she said forthrightly, introducing herself to the boy with a smile and a firm handshake. "Ever work with cattle?"

"No, ma'am," Keith shook his head.

"Well, you'll learn quickly. I can sure use a hand out here. I hope you like the work."

"I think I will," he said.

"That's good, 'cause there's plenty of it." Maris replied with a grin.

"He'll be fine here," Maris assured Jessica.

"I knew that already," Jessica replied. "Thanks, Maris. I hope someone does something as kind for you one day."

"No problem. Come on, Keith, grab your gear and let's get you settled. So long, McCallum, Jessica. Feel free to come out and see him whenever you like. Just call first and make sure we're home."

"I will," Jessica replied.

She watched the two walk off toward the neat, new bunkhouse. The ranch, originally called the Circle W, had been in Maris's husband's family for years. Ray hadn't been the sort of man a woman like Maris deserved. He was a heavy drinker like Keith's father, as well as a gambler and womanizer. Nobody had been surprised when he'd recently come to a bad end—running his pickup into a cement bunker on the highway in a drunken state one night. Maris had been doing all the work on the ranch for years while her lazy husband spent money on foolish schemes and chased the rodeo. It was poetic justice that she ended up with the ranch.

"Hensley's always been a little sweet on her, you know," McCallum confided to Jessica as he drove them back to her place. "It was hard for him to tell her about Ray's death."

"Really? My goodness, she's nothing like his ex-wife."

"Men don't always fall for the same type of woman," he teased. "He called her for me when I approached him about someplace for Keith to go, besides into foster care."

"I'm glad Maris was willing," she said quietly. "Keith's not a bad boy, but he could have ended up in prison so easily, trying to get away from his father."

"It's a hell of a world for kids sometimes," he said.

She straightened the long denim skirt she was wearing with a plaid shirt and boots. "Yes."

He reached over and clasped her hand tightly in his. "I've been thinking."

"Have you? Did it hurt?" she teased.

He chuckled. "Not nice."

"Sorry. I'll behave. What were you thinking?"

His grip eased and he slipped his fingers in between hers. "That Baby Jennifer needs a home and we need a baby."

Thirteen

Jessica had thought about that a lot—that Baby Jennifer needed someone to love her and take care of her. McCallum had been firm about the improbability of a court awarding the baby's care to a single woman. But that situation had changed. She and McCallum were engaged, soon to be married. There was every reason in the world to believe that, under the circumstances, a judge might be willing to let them have custody.

She caught her breath audibly. Bubbles of joy burst inside her. "Oh, Sterling, do you think…!"

His hand grasped hers. "I don't know, but it's worth a try. She's a pretty, sweet baby. And I agree with you—I think our lives would be enriched by having a child to love and raise. There's more to being a mother and father than just biology. It takes love and sacrifice and day-to-day living to manage that." He glanced at her gently. "You aren't the sort of woman who will ever be happy without a baby."

She smiled sadly. "I would have loved to have yours."

"So would I," he replied, his tone as tender as his eyes, which briefly searched hers. "But this is the next best thing. What do you think? Do you want to petition the court for permission to adopt her?"

"Yes!"

He chuckled. "That didn't take much thought."

"Oh, yes, it did. I've thought of nothing else since she was found."

"The judge may say no," he cautioned.

"He may say yes."

He just shook his head. That unshakable optimism touched him, especially in view of all the tragedy Jessica had had in her life. She was amazing. A miracle. He loved her more every day.

"All right, then," he replied. "We'll get a lawyer and fill out the papers."

"Today," she added.

He smiled. "Today."

The wedding of Mary Jo Plumber and Dugin Kincaid was the social event of the decade in Whitehorse. It had all the elements of a Cinderella wedding, except that Mary Jo was a bit past the girlish stage. Nevertheless, she had a designer dress that any princess would have envied. It had a keyhole neckline and a full skirt with yards and yards of satin and imported Belgian lace. The veil trailed back over the long train in a symphony of grace. It was the sort of dress that every young girl dreams of wearing, and Jessica was no exception. She would have loved to have worn that wedding gown.

But being the practical woman she was, she realized that she and Sterling would have to pinch pennies a bit, so an expensive dress was out of the question. It didn't matter, though, she thought as she looked at her handsome fiancé in his dark suit, white shirt and sedate red tie. If she had to be married in a pillowcase with armholes, that would be all right. She loved him so much that nothing else mattered.

The Kincaid ranch had been chosen for the ceremony, rather than any of the small Whitehorn churches. Since it was late June, the weather allowed for an outside wedding, and that was what the Kincaids had planned.

There was a canopy, decorated with orchids that Jeremiah had ordered flown in from Hawaii for the occasion. There were pots of flowers everywhere, and the swimming pool was filled to capacity with floating gardenias. Their scent was delicious.

For the wedding ceremony, chairs had been lined up in front of a lavishly decorated altar flanked by candelabra. No expense had been spared. The reception was being held on the patio of the enormous ranch house, and caterers were already busy setting up tables.

The enormous manicured lawn behind the house was filled to capacity as Mary Jo walked down the aisle toward her husband-to-be. Dugin looked vaguely uncomfortable in his suit, frequently glancing toward his father as if he needed Jeremiah's permission even to get married. It was typical of the way he always bowed to his father's wishes. Dugin had spent most of his life seeking Jeremiah's approval, in one way or another. He'd always been a disappointment to Jeremiah, nevertheless.

The grand piano, brought outside from the living room, was exquisitely played by a local church organist. The wedding march echoed in pure, sweet notes across the lawn, and Mary Jo looked ten years younger in her finery.

She stopped beside Dugin and smiled at him demurely through her veil, Jessica noticed that her hand trembled just before Dugin grasped it, and she was breathing rather quickly. Naturally, she would be nervous, because it was her first marriage. Mary Jo was no spring chicken. Probably she'd never dreamed that she, a children's librarian, would end up married to the son of the richest man in Whitehorn. It was truly a fairy-tale occasion.

The minister presiding at the brief ceremony performed his duties with solemn dignity. Watching the wedding, Jessica thought dreamily of her own forthcoming marriage to Sterling. She lifted her eyes to his when the minister pronounced Dugin and Mary Jo man and wife, and the love in them made McCallum lose track of everything except her radiance.

"I never dreamed of being so happy," she whispered to him, while shouts of glee went up after Dugin had kissed his bride.

"Neither did I," McCallum replied with breathless delight. He touched her face lightly. "You'll be a beautiful bride, Jessie."

"Mary Jo looks gorgeous, doesn't she?" she asked, glancing at the bride. "So pretty—"

A curdling scream cut her off. Everyone else stopped talking, too, and the sudden silence of the bridal party seemed deafening as the scream heightened in pitch and loudness.

"What is it?" someone cried.

McCallum turned instantly, his professional demeanor snapping into place as a woman wearing a caterer's uniform came running toward the crowd.

"It's a man," she cried hysterically. "He's dead, he's dead!"

McCallum moved Jessica gently aside and went to the woman. "Calm down," he said soothingly. "Where is he?"

"Over there," she whimpered. "Behind the oak trees. He's dead…!"

Jeremiah and Dugin Kincaid went with McCallum and a stiff-lipped Sheriff Hensley to a point just beyond the big oaks. A man in a suit was lying faceup on the ground. His eyes were open, staring sightlessly at the blue sky. He had a knife—the kind meat was carved with—sticking out from under his rib cage.

Hensley and McCallum knelt by the body.

Hensley felt around the ears and checked the nails. "Rigor hasn't set in," he stated calmly. "He hasn't been dead long. Skin's not cold." He lifted his head. "Nobody leaves! Lock the front gate and make sure nobody gets out of here," he told McCallum.

"They'll have to get over me first. I'll radio for the coroner and an ambulance."

"Get Bill out here with that fingerprint kit," Hensley added quietly. "If there's a print on that knife, I don't want it smudged. See if someone in the kitchen has some plastic bags."

"On my way," McCallum said. He mentioned for another guest who was a deputy to help him, and stopped to explain to Jessica what had happened. "I'll be back as soon as I can," he added.

"Is it anyone we know?" she asked worriedly.

"No," he replied."I haven't seen him before, and I've been in Whitehorn long enough to recognize a face even if I can't put a name with it. He's a stranger. God knows why he ended up like this." He touched her shoulder. "Try to help us keep people away from there until we get the forensic evidence in hand. It might be the difference between catching the killer or not."

"I'll do what I can."

He nodded and went off to follow the sheriff's orders. The manner in which the man had been killed was disturbing, although he didn't mention that to Jessica. The stabbing was precise enough to indicate that the killer was experienced. It also indicated that the fatal wound had been struck in a most efficient manner—underhanded, not overhanded, and with deadly accuracy. McCallum had investigated murders before. He knew that such proficiency denoted skill. He was hoping against hope that this murder didn't indicate a professional killer was on the loose in Whitehorn.

Two hours later, the forensic evidence was bagged, the medical examiner and the coroner had done their parts and the body had been taken away by ambulance for autopsy at the state crime lab. Hensley had concurred with McCallum's deductions, but that brought them no closer to identifying the killer.

The guests were all closely questioned, but everyone's story seemed to check out. Most troubling was that not one of the guests recognized the murdered man. He was a total stranger, which raised some disquieting questions.

Hensley had to let people go in the end. Mary Jo and Dugin were remarkably patient and understanding about the disruption to what should have been the most memorable day of their lives.

"Imagine that, a murder at my wedding!" Mary Jo said nervously. "What is the world coming to!"

Dugin had his arm around her. "Now, now, honey, let's try not to let it spoil our day."

She looked up at him tearfully. "But it has, don't you see? Oh, why did he have to come here?" She took a steadying breath and lowered her eyes. "After all, nobody even knows who he is!"

"We'll find out," the sheriff said solemnly. "We've got his prints and we'll send them to FBI headquarters back East. If he's ever been in trouble with the law, we'll know his identity."

"I'll bet he has," Mary Jo said coldly. "I'll bet he has! Did you see the way he looked? That cheap suit and that little mustache…"

"Honey, you can't tell a man's character by that," Dugin said indulgently. "Anyway, what would a sweet little lady like you know about such things?"

She straightened her billowing white skirt. "But of course I don't. I was just guessing. Would anyone care for a cold drink? I feel absolutely parched," she said, lightly touching her throat.

When the others declined her offer, Mary Jo wandered over to a bar set up on the wide patio. Jessica watched as she put some ice in a glass, then added a generous pour of liquor. No soda or water, Jessica noticed. The poor woman was obviously more upset than she'd let on. Well, she'd hardly be the first person to reach for a strong drink under stress. Who could blame her? Jessica wondered if she should walk over and say a few words. Then she thought it best to let Mary Jo take a private moment to compose herself.

Mary Jo gave her drink a brief stir, then turned her back to the others and took a deep swallow. The straight bourbon delivered a familiar and satisfying burn. First genuine drink she'd allowed herself all day and it tasted mighty fine. If she had to be kissed, squeezed or oozed over by one or more of these White-horn hicks she would scream. Playing the blushing bride had been more of a strain than she'd expected and she could barely wait for the show to be over. Even though that meant being left alone with her *darling* Dugin.

But Hensley and McCallum hadn't gotten tired yet of playing detective, she noticed. Her dead wedding guest had made their day. Mary Jo smiled to herself, struggling to control her expression. Poor old Floyd, he'd made quite a splash at her party, hadn't he? The man was clearly more interesting dead than alive. That was for sure. How had he ever tracked her down, now that was the mystery. Last she'd seen of Floyd, they were standing before a judge in Denver, and wearing matching bracelets; that lovely police model that comes with a key. But the charges didn't stick and once they'd been released, she and Floyd had a fairly bitter parting.

She'd lived nine lives at least since her days of

running scams with Floyd Oakly. She'd always imagined he was either serving hard time, or dead. Floyd was just a two-bit operator; always was, always would be. Showing up here, for example. Bad move, Floyd. And on her wedding day, of all things. What could he have been thinking of? Didn't he remember how quickly she would pick up whatever he taught her, then show him one better? Thank goodness she'd been able to keep the blood off her dress. Now that would have been a problem. She just didn't know how she managed to handle the stress.

Mary Jo sighed and finished off her drink. She placed the empty glass on the bar and took a deep breath. It looked like the last of her guests were about to go. Wearing a pleasant smile, she started across the patio to say her goodbyes, as a gracious hostess should.

As she joined the group, Jessica smiled and lightly touched her arm. "Feeling better?"

Mary Jo smiled and nodded. "Yes, thanks. I am."

"Don't let it spoil your day, Mary Jo," Jessica said kindly. "It was bad luck that it had to happen here, but you and Dugin have the rest of your lives to be happy together. I hope you both will be."

"Thank you, Jessica. You're so nice." Mary Jo hugged her warmly. "I'm glad you could come."

"So am I."

They left the bridal couple and went back to the car. Jessica looked at McCallum with open concern. He was very quiet, hardly communicative at all as they drove back to town.

"What's wrong?" she asked softly.

"That man," he said. "Why would someone murder him at a wedding? And what was he doing at the wedding in the first place, when not one of the guests knew him?"

"Someone probably did and was afraid to say so," she said.

"That's what I suspect." He sighed heavily. "Jessie, I'm uneasy about the murder. This case has all the earmarks of a professional killer—not a gangland one, but an experienced one, just the same."

"Are you sure?" she asked.

"Oh, yes. I'm sure. The murderer knew exactly how to place that knife. It wasn't an amateur attempt."

"That means that someone at the wedding was a killer," she deduced. "Possibly a professional killer."

He nodded. "That's it."

She sighed heavily. "But this is a small Montana town," she protested. "We're old-fashioned, and people look out for one another...."

"We're part of the modern world, too," he said seriously."And violence has become part of the American experience." He cradled her hand in his as he drove. "Don't worry. There may be a good motive, once we identify him, and it could even turn out to be self-defense."

"You don't think so."

He glanced at her with soft eyes. "Jessica, you

already know me too well. God knows what our lives will be like in twenty years or so."

She smiled brightly. "We'll be just as happy as we are today," she assured him. "And little Jennifer will be in college, or getting married, too."

His fingers contracted around hers. "I hope we have that much time together, and more."

She returned the warm pressure. "So do I."

Their own wedding took place just a few weeks later, in July. They were married in the Whitehorn Methodist Church, with a small group of friends as witnesses. Jessica wore a simple white wedding dress. It had a lace bodice and a veil, even though it was street length, not long and elegant like Mary Jo Plumber's. But when, after their vows, Sterling lifted the brief veil to kiss her, she knew that the dress was completely incidental. The love they shared was the end of the rainbow for her. When his lips touched hers, she laid her hand against his hard, lean cheek and felt tears sliding down her face. Tears of joy, of utter happiness.

Their reception was simplicity itself—the women at the office had baked cookies and a friend had made them a wedding cake. There was coffee and punch at the local community hall, and plenty of people showed up to wish them well.

Finally, the socializing was over. They drove to Jessica's house, where they would have complete privacy, to spend their wedding night. Later, they planned to live at McCallum's more modern place.

"Your knees are shaking," he teased when they were inside, with the door locked. It had just become dark, and the house was quiet—even with Meriwether's vocal welcome—and cozy in its nest of forestland.

"I know," she confessed with a shy smile. "I have a few scars left, I guess, and even now it's all unfamiliar territory. You've been…very patient," she added, recalling his restraint while they were dating. Things had been very circumspect between them, considering the explosive passion they kindled in each other.

"I think we're going to find that this is very addictive," he explained as he drew her gently to him. "And I wanted us to be married before we did a lot of heavy experimenting. We've both suffered enough gossip for one lifetime."

"Indeed we have," she agreed. She reached up to loop her arms around his neck. Her eyes searched his. "And now it's all signed and sealed—all legal." She smiled a little nervously. "I can hardly wait!"

He chuckled softly as he bent is head. "I hope I can manage to live up to all those expectations. What if I can't?"

"Oh, I'll make allowances," she promised as his mouth settled on hers.

The teasing had made her fears recede. She relaxed as he drew her intimately close. When his tongue gently penetrated the line of her lips, she stiffened slightly, but he lifted his head and softly stroked her mouth, studying her in the intense silence.

"It's strange right now, isn't it, because we haven't done much of this sort of kissing. But you'll get used to it," he said in a tender tone. "Try not to think about anything except the way it feels."

He bent again, brushing his lips lazily against hers for a long time, until the pressure wasn't enough. When he heard her breathing change and felt her mouth start to follow his when he lifted it, he knew she was more than ready for something deeper.

It was like the first time they'd been intimate. She clung to him, loving his strength and the exquisite penetration of his tongue in her mouth. It made her think of what lay ahead, and her body reacted with pleasure and eagerness.

He coaxed her hands to his shirt while he worked on the buttons that held her lacy bodice together. Catches were undone. Fabric was shifted. Before she registered the fact mentally, his hair-roughened chest was rubbing gently across her bare breasts and she was encouraging him shamelessly.

He picked her up, still kissing her, and barely made it to the sofa before he fell onto it with her. The passion was already red-hot. She gave him back kiss for kiss, touch for touch, in a silence that magnified the harsh quickness of their breathing.

When he sat up, she moaned, but it didn't take long to get the rest of the irritating obstacles out of the way. When he came back to her, there was nothing to separate them.

Her body was so attuned to his, so hungry for him, that she took him at once, without pain or difficulty, and was shocked enough to cry out.

His body stilled immediately. His ragged breathing was audible as he lifted his head and looked into her eyes, stark need vying with concern.

"It didn't hurt," she assured him in a choked voice.

"Of course…it didn't hurt," he gasped, pushing down again. "You want me so badly that pain wouldn't register now…God!"

She felt the exquisite stab of pleasure just as he cried out, and her mouth flattened against his shoulder as he began to move feverishly against her taut body.

"I love you," he groaned as the rhythm grew reckless and rough. "Jessie, I love you…!"

Her mouth, opened in a soundless scream as she felt the most incredible sensation she'd ever experienced in her life. It was like a throbbing wave of searing heat that suddenly became unbearable, pleasure beyond pleasure. Her body shuddered convulsively and she arched, gasping. He stilled just a minute later, and his hoarse cry whispered endlessly against her ear.

He collapsed then, and she felt the full weight of

him with satisfied indulgence. She was damp with sweat. So was he. She stroked his dark hair, and it was damp, too. Wonder wrapped her up like a blanket and she began to laugh softly.

He managed to lift his head, frowning as he met her dancing eyes.

"You passed," she whispered impishly.

He began to laugh, too, at the absurdity of the remark. "Lucky me."

"Oh, no," she murmured, lifting to him slightly but deliberately. "Lucky *me!*"

He groaned. "I can't yet!"

"I have plenty of time," she assured him, and kissed him softly on the chin. "I can wait. Don't let me rush you."

"Remind me to have a long talk with you about men."

She locked her arms around his neck with a deep sigh. "Later," she said. "Right now I just want to lie here and look at my husband. He's a dish."

"So is my wife." He nuzzled her nose with his, smiling tenderly. "Jessie, I hope we have a hundred more years together."

"I love you," she told him reverently. Her eyes closed and she began to drift to sleep. She wondered how anything so delicious could be so exhausting.

The next morning, she awoke to the smell of bacon. She was in her bedroom, in her gown, with the covers pulled up. The pillow next to hers was dented in and the sheet had been disturbed. She smiled. He must have put her to bed. Now it smelled as if he was busy with breakfast.

She put on her jeans and T-shirt and went downstairs in her stocking feet to find him slaving over a hot stove.

"I haven't burned it," he said before she could ask. "And I have scrambled eggs and toast warming in the oven. Coffee's in the pot. Help yourself."

"You're going to be a very handy husband," she said enthusiastically. She moved closer to him, frowning. "But can you do laundry?"

He looked affronted. "Lady, I can iron. Haven't you noticed my uniform shirts?"

"Well, yes, I thought the dry cleaners—"

"Dry cleaners, hell," he scoffed. "As if I'd trust my uniforms to amateurs!"

She laughed and hugged him warmly. "Mr. McCallum, you're just unbelievable."

"So are you." He hugged her back. "Now get out of the way, will you? Burned bacon would be a terrible blot on my perfect record as a new husband."

"You fed Meriwether!" she gasped, glancing at her cat, who was busy with his own breakfast.

"He stopped hissing at me the second I picked up the can opener," Sterling said smugly. "Now he's putty in my hands. He even likes Mack!"

"Wonderful! It isn't enough that you've got me trained," she complained to the orange cat lying on the floor beside the big dog. Mack was already his friend, "now you're starting on other people!"

"Wait until Jenny is old enough to use the can opener," he said. "Then he'll start on her!"

Jessica looked at him with her heart in her eyes. She wanted the baby so much.

"What if the judge won't let us have her?" she asked with faint sadness.

He took up the bacon and turned off the burner, placing the platter on the table.

"The judge *will* let us have her," he corrected. He tilted up her chin. "You have to start realizing that good times follow bad. You've paid your dues, haven't you noticed? You've had one tragedy after another. But life has a way of balancing the books, honey. You're about due for a refund. And it's just beginning. Wait and see."

"How in the world did a cynic like you learn to look for a silver lining in storm clouds?" she asked with mock surprise.

He drew her close. "I started being pestered by this overly optimistic little social worker who got me by the heart and refused to let me go. She taught me to look for miracles. Now I can't seem to stop."

"I hope you find them all the time now," she said. "And I hope we get Jennifer, too. That one little miracle would do me for the rest of my life. With Jennifer and you, I'd have the very world."

"We'll see how it goes. But you have to have faith," he reminded her.

"I have plenty of that," she agreed, looking at him with quiet, hungry eyes. "I've lived on it since the first time I looked at you. It must have worked. Here you are."

"Here I stay, too," he replied, bending his head to kiss her.

Fourteen

The petition was drawn up by their attorney. It was filed in the county clerk's office. A hearing was scheduled and placed on the docket. Then there was nothing else to do except wait.

Jessica went to work as usual, but she was a different person now that she was married. Her delight in her new husband spilled over into every aspect of her work. She felt whole, for the first time.

They both went out to the No Bull Ranch to see Maris Wyler and Keith Colson. The young man was settled in very nicely now, and was working hard. The homebound teacher who had been working with him since the summer recess was proud of the way he'd pulled up his grades. He was learning the trade of being a cowboy, too, and he'd gone crazy on the subject of wildlife conservation. He wanted to be a forest ranger, and Maris encouraged him. He was already talking about college.

"I couldn't be more delighted," Jessica told McCallum when they were driving back to town. "He's so different, isn't he? He isn't surly or uncooperative or scowling all the time. I hardly knew him."

"Unhappy people don't make good impressions. If you only knew how many children go to prison for lack of love and attention and even discipline.... Some people have no business raising kids."

"I think you and I would be good at it," she said.

He caught the note of sadness in her voice. "Cut that out," he told her. "You're the last person on earth I'd ever suspect of being a closet pessimist."

"I'm trying not to be discouraged. It's just that I want to adopt Jennifer so much," she said. "I'm afraid to want anything that badly."

"You wanted me that badly," he reminded her. "and look what happened."

She looked at him with her heart in her eyes and grinned. "Well, yes. You were unexpected."

"So were you. I'd resigned myself to living alone."

"I suppose we were both blessed."

"Yes. And the blessings are still coming. Wait and see."

She leaned back against the seat with a sigh, complacent but still unconvinced.

* * *

They went to court that fall. Kate Randall was the presiding judge. Jessica knew and liked her but couldn't control her nerves. Witness after witness gave positive character readings about both Jessica and McCallum. The juvenile authorities mentioned their fine record with helping young offenders, most recently Keith Colson. And through it all Jessica sat gripping McCallum's hand under the table and chewing the skin off her lower lip with fear and apprehension.

The judge was watching her surreptitiously. When the witnesses had all been called and the recommendations—good ones—given by the juvenile authorities, she spoke directly to Jessica.

"You're very nervous, Mrs. McCallum," Kate said with teasing kindness and a judicial formality. "Do I look like an ogre to you?"

She gasped. "Oh, no, your honor!" she cried, reddening.

"Well, judging by the painful look on your face, you must think I am one. Your joy in that child, and your own background, would make it difficult for even a hanging judge to deny you. And I'm hardly that." She smiled at Jessica. "The petition to adopt the abandoned baby Jennifer is hereby approved without reservation. Case dismissed." She banged the gavel and stood up.

Jessica burst into tears, and it took McCallum a long time to calm and comfort her.

"She said yes," he kept repeating, laughing with considerable joy of his own. "Stop crying! She may change her mind!"

"No, she won't," the judge assured them, standing patiently by their table.

Jessica wiped her eyes, got up and hugged the judge, too.

"There, there," she comforted. "I've seen a lot of kids go through this court, but I've seen few who ended up with better parents. In the end it doesn't matter that your child is adopted. You'll raise her and be Jennifer's parents. That's the real test of love, I think. It's the bringing up that matters."

She agreed wholeheartedly. "You can't imagine how I felt, how afraid I was," she blurted out.

Kate patted her shoulder. "Yes, I can. I've had a steady stream of people come through my office this past week, all pleading on your behalf. You might be shocked at who some of them were. Your own boss," she said to McCallum, shaking her head. "Who'd have thought it."

"Hensley?" McCallum asked in surprise.

"The very same. And even old Jeremiah Kincaid," she added with a chuckle. "I thought my eyes would fly right out of my head on that one." Kate checked her watch. "I've got another case coming up. You'd better go and see about your baby, Jessica." She dropped the formal address since the court had adjourned. "I expect you new parents will have plenty of things to do now."

"Oh, yes!" she exclaimed. "We'll need to buy formula and diapers and toys and a playpen—"

"We already have the crib," McCallum said smugly, laughing at Jessica's startled reaction. "Well, I was confident, even if you weren't. I ordered it from the furniture store."

"I love you!" She hugged him.

He held her close, shaking hands with the judge.

From the courthouse they went around town, making a number of purchases, and Jessica was in a frenzy of joy as they gathered up all the things they'd need to start life with a new baby.

But the most exciting thing was collecting Baby Jennifer from a delighted Mabel Darren, the woman who'd been keeping her, and taking her home.

Even Meriwether was a perfect gentleman, sniffing the infant, but keeping a respectful distance. Jessica and McCallum sat on the sofa with their precious treasure, and didn't turn on the television at all that night. Instead they watched the baby. She cooed and stared at them with her big blue eyes and never cried once.

Later, as Jessica and McCallum lay together in bed—with the baby's bed right next to theirs instead of in another room—they both lay watching Jennifer sleep in the soft glow of the night-light.

"I never realized just how it would feel to be a parent," McCallum said quietly. "She's ours. She's all ours."

She inched closer to him. "Sterling, what if her mother ever comes back?"

His arms contracted around her. "If her mother had wanted and been able to keep her, we wouldn't have her," he said. "You have to put that thought out of your mind. Sometimes there are things we never find out about in life—and then there are mysteries that are waiting to be solved just around the corner. For instance, we're still working on the mystery murder at the wedding. We may solve it, we may not. The same is true of Jennifer's situation. But we've legally adopted her. She belongs to us, and we to her. That's all there is to it."

Jessica let out her breath in a long sigh. After a minute she nodded. "Okay. Then that's how it will be."

He turned her to face him and kissed her tenderly. "Happy?" he whispered.

"So happy that I could die of it," she whispered back. She pushed her way into his arms and was held tight and close. As her eyes closed, she thought ahead to first steps and birthday parties and school. She'd thought she'd never know those things, but life had been kind. She remembered what McCallum had said to her—that bad times were like dues paid for all the good times that followed. And perhaps they were. God knew, her good times had only just begun!

* * * * *

Presenting

Montana
★ MAVERICKS™

Return to Big Sky country!

YES! Please send me the exciting *Montana Mavericks* collection. This collection will begin with 3 FREE BOOKS and 2 FREE GIFTS in my very first shipment—and more valuable free gifts will follow! My books will arrive in 8 monthly shipments until I have the entire 51-book *Montana Mavericks* collection. I will receive 2 free books in each shipment and I will pay just $4.49 U.S./$5.39 CDN for each of the other 4 books in each shipment, plus $1.99 for shipping and handling.* If I decide to keep the entire collection, I'll only have paid for 32 books because 19 books are free. I understand that accepting the 3 free books and gifts places me under no obligation to buy anything. I can always return a shipment and cancel at any time. My free books and gifts are mine to keep no matter what I decide.

261 HDK 9548 461 HDK 9558

Name	(PLEASE PRINT)	
Address		Apt. #
City	State/Prov.	Zip/Postal Code

Signature (if under 18, a parent or guardian must sign)

Mail to the **Harlequin Reader Service:**

IN U.S.A.: P.O. Box 1867, Buffalo, NY 14240-1867
IN CANADA: P.O. Box 609, Fort Erie, Ontario L2A 5X3

* Terms and prices subject to change without notice. Prices do not include applicable taxes. Sales tax applicable in N.Y. Canadian residents will be charged applicable taxes. This offer is limited to one order per household. All orders subject to approval. Credit or debit balances in a customer's account(s) may be offset by any other outstanding balance owed by or to the customer. Please allow 4–6 weeks for delivery. Offer available while quantities last.

Your privacy: Harlequin is committed to protecting your privacy. Our Privacy Policy is available online at www.eHarlequin.com or upon request from the Reader Service. From time to time we may make our lists of customers available to reputable third parties who have a product or service of interest to you. If you would prefer we not share your name and address, please check here. ☐

MMBPA09

HARLEQUIN®
INTRIGUE®

BREATHTAKING ROMANTIC SUSPENSE

Shared dangers and passions lead to electrifying romance and heart-stopping suspense!

Every month, you'll meet six new heroes who are guaranteed to make your spine tingle and your pulse pound. With them you'll enter into the exciting world of Harlequin Intrigue— where your life is on the line and so is your heart!

THAT'S INTRIGUE— ROMANTIC SUSPENSE AT ITS BEST!

HARLEQUIN®
Live the emotion™

![Harlequin logo] **Harlequin® Historical**
Historical Romantic Adventure!

*Imagine a time of chivalrous
knights and unconventional ladies,
roguish rakes and impetuous
heiresses, rugged cowboys
and spirited frontierswomen—
these rich and vivid tales will
capture your imagination!*

*Harlequin Historical . . .
they're too good to miss!*